Darling Remy,

You would be so pleased, mon cher, to see our youngest daughter working in the kitchen of your restaurant – I know how proud it would make you. Melanie brings her fiery spirit and creative genius to her cooking, and she is perfectly balanced by Robert LeSoeur, our capable new executive chef. Of course, Melanie doesn't see it that way, but between the two of them, Chez Remy is regaining all the excitement and energy that has been missing since we lost you. And who knows? Maybe the sparring in the kitchen between them will lead to sparks of another kind. A mother can't help but hope, and I know you would approve!

I'm trying so hard not to worry about the hotel's precarious financial situation and concentrate on the many things I have to be happy for. The girls and I are counting on this Mardi Gras to set us on a firm footing once again, but with all the recent mishaps, I begin to wonder if more than the madness of the season is at work here. I miss talking to you, Remy, but at least this way I feel that you are near.

All my love,

Anne

Dear Reader,

I started writing this book just after Hurricane Katrina hit. I won't kid you. It was quite difficult writing a romantic fantasy when the reality was so tragic. In order to wrap my head around it so I could write the book, I had to foresee the future and imagine the Crescent City emerging from destruction with courage, dignity and hope.

I offer this book as homage to the old New Orleans that was, and the new New Orleans that will be reborn. As part of that process, I've focused on one of the city's most enduring strengths – the amazing cuisine. The people of New Orleans have a zest for life unlike any other and their spirit is reflected in their food. Food offers both sustenance and comfort. It represents camaraderie and companionship. It is the very fabric of our lives.

So come, break bread with me. Have a beignet and coffee as you read Robert and Melanie's story. Let's toast New Orleans together. *Laissez les bons temps rouler.*

Long live New Orleans.

Much love,

Lori

LORI WILDE
Some Like it Hot

MILLS & BOON®

*First published in Great Britain 2007
by Harlequin Mills & Boon Limited, Eton House,
18-24 Paradise Road,
Richmond, Surrey TW9 1SR*

SOME LIKE IT HOT © by Harlequin Books S.A. 2006

Laurie Blalock Vanzura is acknowledged as the
author of this work.

ISBN: 978 0 263 85855 6

61-0407

*Printed and bound in Spain
by Litografia Rosés S.A., Barcelona*

Lori Wilde is a former registered nurse who now writes romance full-time. When asked what she would do for a living if she couldn't be a romance writer, Lori answers without hesitation – a chef. Her love of food hails back to her childhood when, the oldest of five, she learned to cook when she was eight. Even in these days of fast food and quick-prep packaging, the thing that relaxes Lori most is to prepare a home-cooked meal from scratch for those she loves.

CHAPTER ONE

THE RESTAURANT KITCHEN was hot, but sous-chef Melanie Marchand was hotter.

Thick seafood gumbo simmered on a back burner of the stove. The spicy scent of sweet paprika, cayenne pepper, garlic and onions permeated the air. Dozens of potatoes baked in a five hundred degree oven, while in the convection toaster, fat loaves of French bread turned a buttery golden brown. Chez Remy was in full swing as Mardi Gras season heated up.

Overhead, the ceiling fan was on the fritz, spinning lazily for a few minutes, then abruptly cutting out. Tendrils of dark hair escaped from Melanie's ponytail and perspiration plastered them against the nape of her neck. She pressed the back of one hand to her damp forehead in a useless attempt to stay her irritation.

She'd just glanced up at the daily menu posted on the dry-erase board by executive chef Robert LeSoeur, and noticed that the innovative dish she'd scribbled down the night before had been slashed through with a bright red Magic Marker.

Grrr. She gritted her teeth.

Without even a simple FYI, he'd axed her new specialty dish from the carte du jour, making her feel overlooked and insignificant. The way she'd often felt growing up as the youngest of four sisters. Charlotte was the smart one, Renee the pretty one, Sylvie the funny one. Melanie had just been the baby.

Her cooking skills were the only way she'd been able to distinguish herself. Purposefully, Melanie squared her shoulders, strode to the stainless steel commercial refrigerator and, with her biceps straining, dragged out the forty-pound turkey.

She was making the dish whether Robert liked it or not. He couldn't fire her. Her family owned Chez Remy, the elegant restaurant housed inside the Hotel Marchand, a four-star establishment tucked away on one of the original blocks of the French Quarter.

Ignoring the round-eyed stares of the other cooks, she hauled the turkey over to the prep area. After removing the giblets, she lubed it up with extra virgin olive oil.

The cooks kept glancing from Melanie to the crossed-out menu item posted near the stove, and back again. They recognized mutiny in the offing, but had the good sense not to comment on it. Although Jean-Paul Beaudreau, who had worked for her family since she was a small child, grinned and murmured something in his native Cajun dialect about the sexy appeal of a tempestuous woman.

Humph.

She wasn't tempestuous. She just wanted her voice to be heard. Either LeSoeur simply enjoyed provoking her or the stubborn man needed to be fitted with a high-powered hearing aid. She picked up the oversize bird, now prepped for cooking, and marched it over to the rotisserie.

"It's too big." Robert's voice was a cool caress against her heated ears.

Melanie started, but did not look up at her nemesis because her insides had turned to mush.

Mentally, she steeled herself against the unwanted sensation of sexual attraction by not missing a beat. She kept right on trying to jam the bird into the oven as if Mr. Hot Body himself was not hovering behind her.

"Did you hear what I said?"

A bead of perspiration trickled down her throat. She wasn't about to concede that he was right. Melanie kept working it like Cinderella's ugly stepsister trying to stuff her big fat foot into that delicate glass slipper.

I will make this fit. I can't let him win.

Okay, she was competitive. So shoot her.

"If you're determined to do this, then at least let me help so you don't end up hurting yourself," Robert said softly, and stepped dangerously close.

Who did he think he was fooling? He didn't want to help. He wanted to take over. He thrived on control. She could easily imagine him in the armed forces—a general barking out orders to his troops.

Melanie hardened her jaw. She would not allow this guy to steamroll her.

"Buzz off," she said flatly.

He came up behind her and slid his big arms around either side of her waist, grabbing hold of the slick bird she held positioned in front of her. Suddenly, she was having a lot of trouble breathing normally, and she could not blame it on the heat.

Robert was touching her, and the fact that he was touching her turned her on, and *that* scared the hell out of her.

His warm breath tickled the nape of her neck, his chest grazed her back and his arms rubbed against hers as they struggled together to insert the turkey into the rotisserie.

There was decidedly too much friction going on here.

"Admit defeat gracefully, Marchand," he said after a few minutes of concentrated effort. "It's not going to fit."

"Stop being such a pessimist, and try wriggling it around a bit," she instructed.

He wriggled.

And jiggled.

Nothing happened.

"I told you, it's too big," he gloated.

"Braggart."

"What's that? I don't get an admission that you're wrong and I'm right?"

She could hear the humor in his voice. Was he flirting with her? Or making fun of her?

Underneath his white starched apron, with the maroon Chez Remy stitching across the front, he wore a tight, black cotton T-shirt, black denim jeans and black leather boots. Crocodile, she surmised. Or maybe alligator. Expensive either way. What a shame he could afford better shoes than she could. How much was her mother paying him, anyway?

Not that she was much of a shoe diva, as anyone might have deduced from the scuffed Nikes she wore when she wasn't in her kitchen clogs. She didn't even own a pair of stilettos. She preferred footwear that allowed freedom of movement. She liked to stay fluid, on the go, prepared in case an impromptu adventure broke out. Besides, at five foot nine, she was tall enough that she had no need for high heels.

Weird about Robert, though. In every way except for his footwear, he followed the status quo. Not a rocker of boats, LeSoeur. But those boots whispered, *I do have a wild side even though you can't see it*. That's what intrigued her most about him. This undercurrent, this hidden part of the iceberg.

She cast him a sidelong glance.

Robert caught her looking at him and the right corner of his mouth quirked upward slightly. He was drop-dead gorgeous when he smiled. His posture was cocksure, reflecting the flawless arrogance of a man accustomed to being in charge.

Her knees wobbled.

Benedict Arnold knees.

His smile deepened, showing off a pair of devilish dimples.

Jeez, she was such a fool for dimples. Loved them, in fact.

Melanie jerked her eyes downward and nipped her bottom lip between her teeth in an attempt to focus her attention on the poultry skewering, but the ploy didn't work.

Robert was right. Damn him.

The turkey was much too large for the rotisserie, but she wasn't about to admit she'd been wrong. She would slice off the bird's legs if she had to. One way or another, she was determined to make it fit, because silly as it might sound, she felt as if her entire sense of self hinged on it.

The Hotel Marchand had been faltering ever since Hurricane Katrina, but lately, just as they were getting back on their feet, a series of odd occurrences had been chipping away at their once impeccable reputation. Melanie believed that if she created unique and delicious dishes, people would flock to Chez Remy, boosting the hotel's bottom line. If she could bring in more customers, she would finally feel like an integral part of her family.

But what if you're wrong? What if your passionate creations don't save the day? What if you're always incidental? Lately those doubts had been growing, gnawing at her the way they always did when she'd been in one place too long.

But this is home. You're supposed to be here.

Yeah? So why did she feel so out of step?

Swallowing hard, Melanie slammed the mental door on her demons. This would work if LeSoeur would just kindly move his hunky bod out of her way.

"How long are you going to monkey with that turkey before you admit defeat?" he asked.

"Hush up, Mr. Negativity." Grimly she pounded on the turkey's behind with the flat of her palm. "That's the difference between you and me, LeSoeur. I'm a positive thinker."

"You believe *that's* the biggest difference between us?"

"No, the biggest difference between us is that you're a stick-in-the-mud and I'm an innovator."

"I thought the biggest difference was that you're a hard-headed prima donna who's used to getting her own way and I'm—"

"And you're the guy who's here to put me in my place." She finished his sentence. "Is that it?"

"Melanie," he said. "Your mother and sister hired me as executive chef for a reason. Get used to it. I'm making an executive decision. Chocolate turkey is off the menu."

Defiantly, she lifted her chin. His eyes sparked darkly, letting Melanie know he meant business. The elastic band around her ponytail felt unnaturally tight and her throat was so dry she couldn't swallow. His self-control infuriated her as much as it pointed out her own lack of it.

At two o'clock in the afternoon the kitchen was gearing up for the restaurant's evening opener at five. The three prep cooks were industriously peeling, chopping, slicing and dicing, but they weren't too busy to cast surreptitious glances their way.

Melanie settled the turkey on a Lucite cutting board and wiped her hands against her apron before dropping them onto her hips. From the minute her oldest sister, Charlotte, general manager of the Hotel Marchand, had introduced them to each other four months earlier, Melanie and Robert had been assessing each other's jugular.

Her instant dislike of the man had as much to do with his bossiness—he reminded her far too much of her ex-husband, David—as it did with the fact she found his good looks heart-stoppingly devastating. How was it that she could be so attracted to someone who rubbed her the wrong way on five hundred different levels?

And then there was the not-so-small matter that her mother and Charlotte should have offered the executive chef position to her, rather than bringing in a total stranger.

There was that insignificant feeling again, as if she was nothing but an afterthought. The tag end of the family.

She firmly believed her father, Remy, would have wanted her to have the job if he had still been alive. It was almost four years to the day since he had been killed by a drunk driver in a car crash on Lake Pontchartrain Causeway. An accident that still haunted her because she felt responsible.

Melanie knew her guilt wasn't logical or rational, and she understood that no one in the family blamed her. But she blamed herself. She couldn't help thinking that if she hadn't gotten divorced, hadn't gone through a vicious bout of self-doubt and depression, that her mother, Anne, wouldn't have whisked her away on a two-week vacation to Tuscany to cheer her up during the hotel's busiest time of year.

And if they hadn't been in Italy, Anne would have been

home, and her husband would never have gone out into the storm that horrible, horrible night. Somewhere in the back of her mind, Melanie honestly believed that if she hadn't been an impulsive wild child, disobeying her parents' wishes and marrying David on the spur of the moment and then sorrowfully living to regret it, her father would not have died.

A wave of pain, as gut-wrenching, as when she'd first heard the awful news, washed over her.

Melanie had stayed longer in Tuscany to finish her cooking courses, but, homesick for her husband, Anne had decided to return early. Even now, Melanie could still remember, with perfect clarity, the moment her world had changed forever.

She had been cooking chicken marsala in the quaint, two-hundred-year-old kitchen at Casa Francesco when the call had come through on her cell. Pulling the phone from her apron, she'd spied her oldest sister's number on the caller ID, and was in the middle of making a flippant joke when Charlotte had quietly told her their father was dead.

Melanie had let out a small, keening cry of despair, and the bottle of marsala wine she'd been clutching in her other hand slipped from her fingers, crashing to the cool clay tiles, staining her legs with the ruddy, prune-scented liquid.

She had always been a daddy's girl and far more comfortable here in the working-class world of Remy's kitchen, than in the rest of the hotel, which bore the distinctive markings of her mother's privileged upbringing. Melanie's father had spoiled her something rotten, and she missed him desperately.

Wherever her gaze landed, she saw him.

In the saucepans, bottoms charred black from use. In the stainless steel backsplash they'd installed together behind the stoves, Melanie holding up the metal while her father glued it into place. In the cookbooks stacked on shelves in the corner, their pages yellowed and dog-eared. In the chef knives, gleaming and sharp, that she'd bought him for Christmas the year before he'd died.

Melanie blinked and found she was still staring into Robert LeSoeur's piercing blue eyes. Suddenly, he became the personification of her pain.

And she hated him for it, this tightly muscled, broad-shouldered interloper.

How could her mother and Charlotte have hired a laconic Northwesterner to run her passionate father's kitchen? The betrayal tasted as sharp and raw as undistilled cider vinegar.

She would have already packed her bags and shuffled right on back to Boston if her other two sisters, Sylvie and Renee, hadn't begged her to stay. Plus, how could she hold a grudge against her mother? Anne's recent heart attack was the reason Melanie had returned to New Orleans again. Even though the myocardial infarction had been mild and Anne insisted she felt better than ever now, Melanie could not bear the thought of losing another parent.

So she'd sucked up her resentment and decided to play nice with Robert, but the turkey was the last straw. Whenever she made any suggestions for trying something new or innovative, he invariably shot her down with his rational, logical, well-thought-out opinions.

"I repeat, Melanie, I'm in charge. This is my kitchen. We're frying the turkey Cajun style. End of discussion."

She didn't flinch from his assessing gaze. "Everything on the frickin' menu is Cajun or Creole."

His eyes traveled a deliberate journey from her disheveled hair down her face to her lips, along her throat to the gentle swell of her breasts. "Hello, this is New Orleans, not Boston."

"But why does everything have to be so predictable?" she complained. "Same old gumbo and étouffée. I have rémoulade coming out of my pores."

"There's nothing wrong with tradition," he said. "People find it soothing."

"Yeah, if you don't mind stagnating. What are the more adventuresome souls supposed to eat?"

"Few people are as adventuresome as you." Was that a hint of admiration in his voice? Perhaps he did appreciate her love of innovation more than he let on. "And for what it's worth, I have introduced more grilled dishes since I've been here."

Melanie snorted. "Grilled grouper, whoop-dee-doo. That'll get you on the cover of *Gourmand*."

"This isn't about making the cover of some slick foodie magazine. It's about pleasing our customers. Besides, roast turkey is not exactly cutting edge."

"It is when you baste it with chocolate and cayenne, then top it with a goat cheese and caper sauce." She gestured expressively. "Don't make that face, it tastes really good."

"You've made it before?"

"It came to me in a dream. I have very vivid dreams."

"We can't be switching the menu around to suit your midnight culinary inventions. The dish sounds dysfunctional. No one will order it."

"Trust me—it's wonderful." Melanie turned resolutely back to the turkey. She grasped the bird under both wings and lugged it back to the rotisserie to try again.

Robert moved to block her way. "Sorry, but no. It'll fry in less than half the time."

The kitchen had gone completely silent. The trio of prep cooks were no longer slicing and dicing, but staring open-mouthed, waiting with knives poised to see what was going to happen next.

Melanie couldn't say why getting her way on this issue was so important, but the need was an aching heaviness in her heart. Maybe because the anniversary of her father's death was just around the corner. Maybe because her own family didn't have enough faith in her to give her the executive chef position. Not that she even wanted the job, but it would have been nice of them to have asked. It would have made her feel wanted, at least.

Or maybe it was because no matter how much she disliked Robert, she was powerfully attracted to him and feared she would end up sleeping with the guy and making a huge mess of her life again if she didn't watch her step.

Melanie dodged around him and manipulated the turkey's shoulders into the rotisserie. If she just pushed hard enough, she could make it happen.

"You're going to hurt yourself," Robert said, and reached for one of the legs.

"Back off," she barked, surprised by the anxiety knotting her stomach.

"You're upset about something more than the turkey. Let's go into my office and talk this through."

The last place she wanted to be was confined in his tiny office. She didn't trust herself to be alone with him. How pathetic was that?

"No."

Robert tried to wrench the turkey from her grasp, but

Melanie clung to it as if her life depended on it being roasted in chocolate and hot peppers instead of injected with Cajun seasoning and fried in peanut oil. In the process, her elbow hit the jar of olive oil, tipping it over. Apparently, she hadn't replaced the lid tightly enough. Oil drizzled down the counter and trickled across the floor.

"Let go," she said.

"Not until you tell me what's really upsetting you."

Melanie glared. She wasn't about to tell him that what was really bothering her was this infernal attraction to him. She pulled away sharply, but still he held on to the turkey.

Her kitchen clogs skidded in the slippery oil. Her legs shot out from under her and she landed hard on her bottom, the turkey flying from her hands and Robert's.

It smacked against something in the distance with a solid, wet thunk.

Robert let out a curse as momentum shot him forward and he, too, slipped in the olive oil, lost his balance and came crashing down.

Just in the nick of time he thrust out his arms and caught himself before crushing Melanie beneath him.

He ended up positioned directly above her as if he were doing push-ups, her legs pinned beneath his.

She froze.

He gazed down at her with those deep, ocean-colored eyes. Her chest heaved beneath the thin cotton material of her turquoise tank top.

She was trapped.

And totally not hating it.

In fact, Melanie was holding her breath, waiting for him to kiss her.

His hands rested on either side of her body, his forearms almost grazing the swell of her breasts, his pelvis poised just inches above hers.

She realized that somehow his fingers had gotten tangled in her ponytail, and he was looking at her as if she were a Mardi Gras feast.

She gulped and commanded herself not to blush.

Her body tingled, sparking off the hot expression in his eyes. Her stomach tumbled in a free fall. The way he looked at her was foreplay of the most provocative kind.

Hot and lingering. Anticipatory and edgy.

Her heart raced like a high-performance Ferrari engine. She tipped her hips forward.

They breathed deeply together, watching, waiting.

For the first time, she noticed he had a faint scar that started just above his right ear and disappeared into his hairline. It was straight and clean, as if it had been made by a razor or a knife in one long slicing motion.

Something shifted inside her. Something brilliant and bright and inexplicable.

She had a scar of her own.

It seemed portentous somehow, his scar. A harbinger of things to come. A warning. And she knew it held a secret to which she wasn't privy.

She had no conscious intention of touching it, but touch it she did, reaching up to feather one finger along the outer border.

He'd suffered.

Just as she had.

Quick as a kid who'd poked a lit match, Melanie jerked her fingers back, afraid of the intimacy. Wanting the connection, but terrified of it.

His lips parted, and for one crazy, glorious moment she thought he *was* going to kiss her. But instead, he simply asked, "Are you all right?"

"Get off me."

Rattled by an inexplicable need to bond with this man, she pushed against his chest with the flat of one palm, when what she really wanted to do was snatch the front of his T-shirt in her fist and pull his body down flush against hers.

One of the prep cooks snickered.

Robert scrambled to his feet, shot a quelling glance at the curious trio and then reached down a hand to help her up.

But Melanie would be damned if she would take any help from him. Ignoring his outstretched palm, she sprang effortlessly to a standing position. She didn't run four miles a day and do strength training exercises twice a week for nothing.

She looked around for the turkey. Robert's gaze followed hers. The bird had landed with freaky precision on a hook where the staff hung their aprons when they went outside for a break.

It dangled there, a testament to her failure.

Melanie's eyes met Robert's. He pressed his lips together, suppressing a grin.

It *was* funny, but she refused to laugh, refused to encourage him.

"I was going to offer to let you design the stuffing," Robert said, his eyes dancing, "but looks like it's a moot point, since the turkey's been hung out to dry."

"You know what you can do with your stuffing," she said sweetly, taking off her apron and tossing it at him.

Then without another word, she pivoted on her heel and

marched out the employee entrance, trying not to let him see how much he disturbed her equilibrium.

Clearly, it wasn't the turkey that didn't fit at Chez Remy. It was her.

CHAPTER TWO

TOUCHING MELANIE HAD BEEN a grave mistake, and Robert knew he shouldn't have done it. Not only was it unprofessional, but it shot his desire for her right out of firing range.

What in the hell had he been thinking?

You weren't thinking. That's the problem.

He was holding the apron she'd tossed at him, caught in midair and clutched tight in his fist. It smelled of food and Melanie, two of his favorite scents.

Suppressing a guttural sound of animal appreciation, Robert pressed his lips together as he watched her storm from the kitchen.

What a woman.

The kind of woman who could get a man into deep trouble without even trying.

You don't need the hassle.

Melanie put him in mind of rich French truffles—precious and musky, heavy with the fragrance of a rumpled mattress after a night of torrid love. Robert would be lying to himself if he didn't admit that she was the source of the buzzy tingling at the base of his brain. He had an overwhelming desire to yank her into his bed and make slow, hot love to her all night long.

The sunlight streaming through the back door as she

jerked it open gave a golden glow to her skin. She possessed nicely defined muscles—developed from years of lifting forty-pound turkeys—over slender bones. Her ebony hair swung in a thick ponytail, and her perfectly shaped tush twitched enticingly in those skin-hugging blue jeans.

No one, but no one, had a caboose like Melanie Marchand's. The image of her cute little butt was branded into his brain.

Stop it! You've got no business lusting after her. She's far too good for the likes of you.

The door slammed, putting an end to the delightful view, but not his wicked thoughts. The very essence of her—zesty, tangy, rebellious—lingered in the resulting backdraft of air.

"Back to work." He frowned and clapped his hands at the prep cooks, not wanting them to guess exactly how much he'd been affected by his close encounter of the dangerous kind with the sexy Ms. Marchand.

In movements so simultaneous they appeared choreographed, the three men picked up their knives and attacked the vegetables on the chopping block with renewed fervor.

Robert removed the bedraggled turkey from the apron hook and cleaned up the mess. After he finished, he left the kitchen for his office, on the other side of the supply pantry, trying to decide the best way to handle Melanie.

You're not going to handle her at all. She's strictly hands-off.

She would be back to finish her shift. He had no worries on that score. Melanie was a professional. She just needed some cooling-off time, and he would give her as wide a berth as possible. He realized she begrudged him for being in charge of the kitchen that had once been the domain of her beloved father. Robert knew he sparked her cantankerous side because several Marchand employees and family members had already told him so.

But he also realized that Melanie secretly lusted after him as much as he lusted after her. He'd watched her nipples stiffen beneath her cotton tank top when his hand had accidentally grazed her breast. He'd seen the expression in her eyes, had felt that magical tug of their sexual push-pull, and it scared her as much as it scared him.

Melanie was a spicy one, and that was precisely the danger of her. Robert shook his head. He knew better than to indulge his fantasies. He'd learned the hard way that too much passion invariably led to disaster.

Just thinking about her lips—as full and pinky-orange as fresh summer peaches—stirred him. He loved her spunk and respected the way she didn't let anyone push her around.

Including him.

Yet the vivacious woman seemed to have no clue about the hunger he held tightly harnessed, the yearning that challenged his self-control long after she'd left the building. He closed his eyes tight against a sudden image of her sprawled out naked across his bed while he skimmed his tongue over her bare breasts and she moaned softly for more.

He opened his eyes, shocked by the sheer force of his desire, disturbed by how much she unbalanced him. He was in way over his head.

Robert was far too familiar with the perils of uncontrollable appetites. That's why he held back. He would not screw this up. He'd worked hard to repair his damaged reputation.

Anne and Charlotte Marchand had given him his big break, offering him the kitchen to run as he saw fit, giving him a chance at a new beginning, a new chapter in his life. He wasn't about to let them down.

And he wasn't about to start something he couldn't finish with Melanie.

Robert dropped down into the rolling swivel chair behind the ornate mahogany desk and did the one and only thing he knew would tame the long-buried needs demanding to be recognized. He unlocked the top drawer of his desk, removed his leather-bound journal and began to write, draining his feelings from his body, channeling them through his pen, detailing his red-hot attraction to Melanie on the page.

If there was one thing he'd learned, it was to stay away from uncontrollable passion. Melanie Marchand was strictly off-limits.

HOW WAS SHE EVER GOING to convince Robert to give her creative reign in the kitchen? Melanie paced the courtyard outside the restaurant, her mind in hyperdrive. It was the only way she could carve her own niche. The only way she could measure up.

Face it. He's in charge and he's convinced he knows best.

She sighed.

If you can't convince him, maybe you can find a way to get rid of him, whispered her darker side.

But how?

Her mother and sisters adored the guy, as did the rest of the staff. He was a fair boss; Melanie couldn't fault him on that score. Days off were decided by lottery, and scullery duty was rotated among the junior staff members. But overall, he was simply too rigid and duty bound.

Robert held part of himself in reserve, never fully giving in to his creativity. He was a great administrator, but Chez Remy was never going to regain its legendary status under his rule if he didn't learn to let go and take some risks.

If she could find out more about him, maybe then she could understand him. And if she understood what made him tick, maybe she could convince him to trust her culinary instincts. Together they could skyrocket Chez Remy—and the Hotel Marchand—to a whole new level.

Then, finally, her mother and sisters would have to recognize that she *was* an integral part of this family.

Restlessly, she toyed with her watch. It had been a present from her father for her eighteenth birthday.

Melanie released the clasp and flipped it over to read the inscription she knew by heart. To my little rebel. Love, Papa.

Her fingertips lightly traced the words and her heart pinched. Being a rebel might have served her in her youth, when she was trying to stand out among her three older sisters, but now, as she neared thirty, she no longer relished the role of outcast. How did a prodigal daughter go about proving that she could indeed go home again?

By restoring her papa's kitchen to its former glory days, that was how.

But how could she do that when Robert was standing in her way?

Melanie slipped her watch back on and then unclipped her cell phone from the waistband of her blue jeans. Taking a deep breath, she flipped the phone open and punched in the number of an old friend who worked at one of the top restaurants in Seattle, Robert's hometown.

If anyone could dig up scuttlebutt, it was Coby Harrington. Coby was the biggest gossip on the Pacific Rim, plus he owed her a huge favor.

Five years ago, when they'd both been working for her ex-husband, David, in Boston, Melanie had saved his bacon. Coby mistakenly put peanuts in a Thai dish for one of their regulars, a member of a well-known political clan, who was highly allergic to the nuts. When Melanie realized Coby's mistake, she'd rushed out into the dining area, knocking the plate from the waiter's hand just as he was about to serve it to the customer.

She'd taken the brunt of her ex-husband's wrath over the incident, and never mentioned Coby's error. She'd known David would have fired him on the spot.

"Coby? This is Melanie Marchand."

"Toots, is it really you? Long time, no hear. How have you been?"

"I'm fine. You?"

"Delicious as always."

Melanie chuckled at her flamboyant friend. "Good to hear."

"How's your mother?"

"She's recovering just fine, thanks for asking. Listen, Coby, I need a really big favor."

"What's up?"

"Could you put your ear to the ground and see what you can find out about a Robert LeSoeur? He used to be an assistant executive chef at the Stratosphere."

"Hmm, is he a new love interest?"

"No, nothing like that."

"That's a shame. When are you going to get over that brute David and move on?"

"Please, I'm so over David."

"Then how come you haven't had a boyfriend since the divorce? It's been more than four years."

It was a legitimate question, but she hadn't found anyone who piqued her interest enough to try again.

What about Robert? whispered that infernal voice in the back of her brain.

"Once burned, twice shy," she said. "I don't exactly have the world's best track record when it comes to picking men."

"You're too passionate to be alone," Coby commented. "You can't let old war wounds stop you from trying again."

"I'll try again when the right guy comes along. I've learned my lesson. I'm taking it slow this time."

"Fair enough. So you want me to dig up deep dirt on this LeSoeur character?"

"Well, yes, if there's any deep dirt to be dug."

"Honey," he said, "everyone has a bone or two in their closet, if not an entire skeleton. If he's done it, I'll find it. But first, you wanna tell me what this is really all about?"

"He's a new employee at the restaurant and we don't know much about him."

"There's something you're not telling me. Quid pro quo, Mel. You dish, I snoop."

"Hey, you owe me. Remember what happened at Culligan's in Boston?"

"I already repaid you for that one, toots. I kept your dark secret."

He had at that, and keeping secrets was not Coby's forte. Reflexively, Melanie's hand went to her left side, her fingers skating over the uneven ridge of the burn scar that lay underneath the thin material of her tank top.

Closing her eyes, she bit her lip, refusing to relive the

memory of how David, in a cocaine-induced rage, had shoved her against a gas stove that had been turned on at the time. Coby was the only one in the whole world who knew about it. Melanie had been too ashamed to tell her family, because she'd married a man she'd known less than a month. A man they'd disapproved of. The very day after the stove incident, Melanie had moved out and filed for divorce, but she still hadn't shaken the shame.

"Talk to me," Coby prodded.

She cast a glance over her shoulder at the kitchen entrance and dropped her voice to a whisper. "I think someone on the inside might be trying to damage the Hotel Marchand's reputation, and it all started about the same time Robert came to work for us."

"I'm listening."

"Keep this just between you and me."

"You got it."

"There've been several strange happenings around here," she said.

"Happenings?"

"Someone put granulated sugar in the feed line to the hotel generator so we were without power during a city-wide blackout and guest rooms were vandalized. Then someone tipped off the paparazzi about a movie star guest, and that was followed by a hit-and-run."

She winced, remembering the car accident she'd been in two weeks earlier involving her three-year-old niece, Daisy Rose, and director Pete Traynor's four-year-old nephew, Adam. Luc Carter, the hotel concierge, had been driving them in her grandmother Celeste's cadillac. A black sedan with tinted windows had come out of nowhere, smacking their vehicle before speeding off without stopping. They'd been shaken up, but everyone was okay. Both Melanie and Luc were convinced the crash had been intentional, but there was no way to prove it.

The police suspected paparazzi on the hunt were behind the accident. Pete Traynor was in town to scout out a location for his next flick, and had brought his nephew along. His art director, Evan, was also with him, plus Evan's fiancée, a famous Australian actress named Ella Emerson. It was news of their secret wedding that was leaked to the press.

The family was still on edge over the accident and Melanie couldn't dispel the feeling that the hit-and-run was somehow connected to the other attacks on the hotel. But even if Robert was behind any of those, she knew in her heart that he couldn't be involved in the hit-and-run. In spite of his faults, he adored Daisy Rose and would never do anything to harm her.

"Okay, you got my attention. I'll get on it and call you back as soon as I find out something," Coby said.

Melanie thanked her friend and hung up, telling herself she'd done the sensible thing, even as her stomach took a nosedive into her shoes.

No matter how prudent it seemed, she couldn't help feeling that having Robert investigated, however secretly, was a very underhanded thing to do.

DAWN RODE THE Saturday morning sky, gray and edgy. Robert ambled down the aisles of the open-air market, looking for the freshest ingredients for Chez Remy's evening menu.

He hadn't slept much the night before. He kept thinking of Melanie and how to improve their working relationship without giving in to sexual temptation. Yesterday, she'd come back inside a few minutes after their argument, going about her job as if nothing had happened. Robert stayed out of her way, but the more he thought about it, the more he knew he was going to have to sit her down for a serious heart-to-heart.

Something had to be done about the escalating tension between them, because Robert had no intention of leaving the best job he'd ever had or the city of New Orleans, which he'd come to love as much as his hometown of Seattle. Even in the midst of its reconstruction from Hurricane Katrina, it had a spirit and energy he found engaging.

Maybe it was because New Orleans was a town that embraced its passionate side, something Robert himself had trouble doing. Or perhaps the town's let-the-good-times-roll philosophy held a promise he wanted to believe in.

He felt it then. The old bump of despair and the familiar sadness that had driven him from Seattle, feelings that he thought he'd conquered. They'd almost disappeared here in the Crescent City, but today in the crowded market, loneliness suddenly crashed down on him without warning.

One minute he was assessing crawfish and thinking about Melanie Marchand, and the next, the heavy weight was upon him.

It had caught him like that before, a thick fist squeezing the air from his lungs.

A flash of images tripped across his brain. Nine years old, he saw his mother walking out the door. She had a suitcase in one hand and a man he didn't know in the other. Tears streaked her face. Her goodbye kiss left a lipstick imprint on Robert's cheek.

"Don't!" he growled aloud. *Push through it. You know how. It'll pass.*

"Pardon?"

"Nothing." He forced himself to take a deep breath and shake off the gloom. He met the fishmonger's eyes and ordered fifty pounds of crawfish to be delivered to the hotel.

"Excuse me, but aren't you Robert LeSoeur?"

Robert turned his head to find a petite young blonde smiling at him. He was accustomed to women flirting with him on the street. It happened a lot. While he didn't consider himself a particularly handsome man—his chin was too prominent and his nose crooked, and he was just a tad bowlegged—women seemed to hold a different opinion. He'd been told he had a strong jaw and a rugged nose and the sexiest walk they'd ever seen. In addition, they went gaga over his dimples and were intrigued by his scar. Would they be so intrigued, he often wondered, if they knew how he'd gotten it?

He didn't recognize the woman. Not at first. But she was very easy on the eyes, and since he was trying hard to stop thinking sexual thoughts about Melanie, he smiled back at her. "Do we know each other?"

"You don't remember me."

He shook his head. "I'm sorry, no."

"We used to take the same ferry into Seattle from Whidbey Island."

"Yes." He did remember her now. "Your hair was longer back then."

"And I was a bit thinner." She laughed and patted her stomach. "The food in New Orleans definitely agrees with me."

"I'm sorry," Robert murmured. "I don't recall your name."

She extended a hand. "Jeri Kay Loving. I'm a reporter for the *Times-Picayune*."

Robert groaned, then immediately apologized. "I'm sorry. That was rude."

Jeri Kay grinned ruefully. "Please, don't be embarrassed, I get that reaction a lot. Comes with the territory."

"This wasn't an accidental meeting."

"No," she admitted. "So tell me, Robert, as one old friend to another, what's behind the rumors about the Hotel Marchand?"

MELANIE JOGGED ALONG the path of the Mississippi River, feeling cranky from not getting enough sleep. She'd spent the night tossing and turning and mentally cursing Robert. It was bad enough she had to deal with his sexiness at work, but now the guy had the audacity to show up in her dreams, cocking that dimpled grin of his and ordering her around.

Except that in her X-rated midnight fantasy she hadn't minded his bossiness.

A shiver flashed through her as she remembered the dream.

She hadn't been asleep long, maybe an hour, when Robert came swaggering into her bedroom looking absolutely gorgeous. His grin said, *I know I turn your insides into instant pudding.*

Even in her slumber, he had a way of looking at her that made her feel both breathless and brainless.

A deadly combo.

Melanie shook her head to get rid of the memory. She veered to her left, sprinting past the open-air market, bustling with more activity than usual now that the Mardi Gras season had begun.

She shouldn't have been surprised to see Robert—this was where the city's chefs came to shop after all. But for some reason, when she spotted him in the milling crowd, her stomach lurched.

And then she realized why.

He was talking to a petite, yet voluptuous, blond woman. His head was down and he was nodding intently, hanging on her every word.

Jealousy, ugly and bile-green, ripped through Melanie.

She didn't like feeling this way. But there it was. She hated seeing him standing so close to another woman.

Idiot, she chided herself. *You don't even like the guy. Why are you getting jealous over him?*

The woman turned in her direction. Melanie recognized her, and her jealousy morphed into suspicion.

It was one of those nosy reporters who had been snooping around for the past couple of weeks, ever since someone had tipped off a celebrity tabloid magazine that Ella Emerson was staying at the Hotel Marchand. Melanie's mother and Charlotte hadn't wanted to think that someone on staff was the source of the leak.

Could Robert be the culprit who'd tipped off the press about Ella? But what on earth was his motive? Why would he want to harm the hotel?

Keeping her back turned, Melanie inched down the produce aisle toward them.

Robert and the reporter were deep in conversation. They probably wouldn't even notice her, and if Robert did see her, she would simply pretend she was shopping and hadn't spied him.

She picked up a plump cantaloupe from a stand on the

opposite side of the aisle where he and the woman stood, heads together, murmuring in low, conspiratorial tones. Melanie raised the melon to her nose and inhaled its sweet scent.

What if Robert wasn't leaking anything, and she was interrupting his romance? The two of them did seem quite cozy.

Jealousy took another stab at her.

Did she really want to hear them coo sweet nothings to each other? No, she didn't, but she was eavesdropping anyway.

Melanie tilted her head, straining to hear their conversation. And then she heard Robert speak her name.

What was that?

Tentatively, she edged closer. He possessed a deep, richly resonant voice that matched his controlled demeanor damn near perfectly. It made it easier for Melanie to distinguish his speech from the babble around her.

"The press leak was dealt with and we're all gearing up for a great Mardi Gras at the hotel," Robert said.

Hmm, he sounded like he was a PR rep for the hotel not its executive chef. Her feelings were conflicted, part pride and relief, part suspicion and surprise.

Maybe he knew she was eavesdropping and he was faking it for her sake.

The reporter said something that Melanie couldn't hear. Customers flowed around her, and the buzz of voices speaking with different accents made her lose Robert's. She took another step closer and then another, all the while keeping her back to Robert and his companion.

"You want to know what I think is going on at the Hotel Marchand?" Robert asked the woman.

Maybe she'd given him too much credit too soon. Melanie

decided. She peered over her shoulder, waiting to hear what he would say next.

"What?" the reporter asked breathlessly, gazing up at him with obvious sexual interest.

He murmured something, took the reporter's elbow and guided her through the crowd, away from Melanie.

Damn it. She started after them, but someone clamped a tight fist on her wrist.

Startled, Melanie looked up to find a disgruntled vendor frowning at her.

"You gonna buy the cantaloupe, lady? Or do I have to call the cops?"

CHAPTER THREE

"I'LL PAY FOR HER MELON."

Robert's voice, deep and downright delicious, came from directly behind her. Melanie closed her eyes and stifled a groan.

Busted.

She opened her eyes to see him pass a couple of dollars to the fruit vendor for her cantaloupe. Her gaze trailed up the sleeve of his blue plaid shirt to his broad shoulders and then on to his eyes.

In the early morning light those eyes glistened almost navy-blue. Normally, they were the intriguing color of an Indian summer sky, although, occasionally, when he wore a pale-colored shirt, they lightened to sweet cerulean.

Chameleon eyes. Intense, powerful. They fascinated her.

Amusement was in them now and she knew that he had caught her eavesdropping.

"I was just out jogging," she said, indicating her running attire with the wave of a hand.

He took his time looking, cocking his head and trailing his gaze over the tight fit of her Lycra workout pants. "And you decided to stop off and steal a cantaloupe for breakfast?"

"I wasn't stealing."

"No?" He arched an eyebrow. Why did he have to look so damn good?

"Of course not."

He was teasing her and she knew it, but Melanie couldn't help fretting that he would think her capable of stealing. She was disconcerted to realize she valued his opinion of her. When had that happened?

Passersby jostled them. Robert took her arm and drew her out of the way of the foot traffic.

Her pulse quickened at his touch.

Calm down, she scolded herself.

"What *were* you doing?" he drawled, and half lowered his eyelids in a sultry, just-rolled-out-of-bed look. Oh, he knew all right. He was just toying with her.

She shrugged. She wasn't good at lying.

"You were trying to listen in on my conversation with Jeri Kay Loving," he said. "Confess."

"Who?" She feigned ignorance.

"The reporter from the *Times-Picayune*?"

"Oh, was that who she was?"

"Don't play dumb. You're too smart for that. Were you spying on me?" His tone was totally seductive.

Flustered, Melanie felt the flush of embarrassment push hotly up her neck, but then she realized she didn't have to explain herself to him. He was the one who'd been talking to a reporter.

Robert took a step closer, crowding her space, marking his territory. His heated gaze seared her to the spot and one corner of his mouth quirked up, taunting her to admit she'd been snooping. Melanie did not shrink back. She wasn't going to let him intimidate her with his overt masculinity.

"Or perhaps you were stalking me?"

"Please, don't flatter yourself."

"Spying it is, then."

"Why would you assume I was spying? Do you have something to hide?" She answered his question with some of her own.

"Why would you even ask that?"

"You're pretty secretive, LeSoeur. You don't talk about yourself much. Why is that?"

"I'm a quiet guy."

"You weren't too quiet just now, talking to that reporter."

"What are you suggesting?"

"Are you the reason the paparazzi found out about Ella Emerson?" Melanie narrowed her eyes at him. "Are you our leak?"

"No," he said, lowering both his voice and his head until he was close enough to brush his lips against her ear if he chose to do so. "I'm not."

Her knees liquefied. In spite of the cool morning air and a strong desire to shiver, she felt blazingly hot. "I don't believe you."

His chin lightly grazed her cheek. The man had a jaw like a rock ledge. A very steep, very slippery, very dangerous ledge. Melanie tried not to notice how his warm breath fanned the fine hairs at the nape of her neck, sending a dangerous jolt of heat flashing through her.

"Well," Robert said, "I guess you're going to have to trust me then."

"I didn't just fall off a turnip truck, buddy. Trusting strangers isn't my long suit."

"We're not strangers," he argued. "We've been working together for four months."

"And yet I don't know a single personal thing about you."

"What would you like to know?" He leaned against a support pillar and flashed his dimples at her.

She thought about it a moment. "How old were you when you lost your virginity?"

"Wow, you hop right to the really intimate stuff."

She could tell by the look on his face that her question had caught him off guard. That had been her intention. "Just answer the question."

"Why don't we start with something easier, like what's my favorite color?"

"You favorite color wouldn't tell me anything important about you. Besides, I can guess. It's blue. Or black, maybe."

"How did you know?"

"Those are the colors you wear most."

"So by that reasoning your favorite color is purple."

"Answer the question," she insisted.

"It's the virginity story or nothing?"

She shrugged. "If you want me to trust you, then you're going to have to share."

"I'll tell you if you'll tell me," he teased.

"I'm not the secretive one."

"Tit for tat."

"Okay, fine. I'm not embarrassed. I was one month shy of seventeen," she said glibly. "It happened on a riverboat with a twenty-two-year-old trumpet player named Johnny Maxx, during Sylvie's college graduation party. The band was playing "My Prerogative." While my parents and sisters were dancing in the ballroom, Johnny and I were on the upper deck underneath a scratchy woolen blanket. He was a thoroughly bad boy, that Johnny. He blabbed about it later to all his Bourbon Street buddies."

"I'm feeling the urge to hunt down Johnny Maxx and punch him in the mouth."

"That's so sweet of you." She fluttered her eyelids. "But don't worry. I wasn't that vulnerable. I wasn't in love with him. I knew what I was getting myself into with Johnny. I just wanted a little fun."

Robert reached up to finger a strand of her hair that had escaped from her ponytail. "You always have to play the tough girl, huh? Come on, you can admit it to me. Johnny Maxx might not have broken your heart, but he hurt your pride."

Robert was right. Johnny had hurt her badly.

"Have you always done that?" he asked.

"Done what?"

"Said and done things strictly for shock value?"

His insight surprised her, but she didn't answer the question. "So what's *your* lost virginity story?"

"Nothing special."

"I need details, man."

He gave her a wry smile and shook his head. "You won't let go of this."

"Nope. What was her name?"

"Amber Jenson. Her father owned a string of dry cleaners."

"Did you do it in the back of one of those hot, steamy rooms where they press the clothes?"

"No. I told you it was nothing special. We were on her parents' living room sofa. Like you, I was barely seventeen. And just to gain your trust, I'm going to admit to the truly embarrassing part." He paused.

"What's that?"

"Um, let's just say things went off a bit prematurely."

Melanie laughed, delighted that he'd revealed his youthful vulnerability to her. "Was Amber disappointed?"

"Terribly."

"I hope you've corrected that problem since then."

"Absolutely."

The suggestive look he gave her made Melanie regret starting this little game.

"All right. No guy would cop to that if it wasn't true. I believe you. So what did you tell the reporter?"

"She'd heard rumors of the hotel's recent problems so I gave her an explanation that seemed to satisfy her."

"Such as?" Melanie asked, fixating on the blunt, fascinating shape of his mouth.

"I told her the Hotel Marchand is haunted."

"You didn't."

"I did." He looked inordinately proud of himself.

"What'd you say?"

"That there was a restless poltergeist. The ghost of a long-dead Creole Queen who'd hanged herself after being spurned by her married lover."

"Pretty good, but personally, I would have gone with the ghost of the spurned married lover, who died a horrible death after the Creole Queen put a voodoo hex on him. But then that's just me. I will have to give you brownie points for creativity, however."

"I have more imagination than you give me credit for." He tilted his head and sent her an assessing glance. "You're not the only one who has vivid dreams."

The way he said it suggested his midnight fantasies had been as erotic as her own. Melanie's stomach tightened at the idea. Was she in his dreams the way he'd been in hers? The thought was both thrilling and unsettling.

"Too bad you don't show as much creativity when it comes to designing your menus," she said saucily, anxious to hide her discomfort.

"Ah," he said. "So it's back to that."

"We're always going to be back to that. Cooking is not only my career, it's my passion. It's the way I express myself."

"Contrary to your opinion, Chez Remy doesn't exist solely so you can express yourself."

She shifted the melon from one hand to the other, then tucked it under her arm. "If we worked together instead of against each other, with your management expertise and my cooking skills, Chez Remy could be one of the top restaurants in the country."

"I agree."

She blinked. "You do?"

"I agree that working together would make things go a lot smoother in the kitchen, and we wouldn't have turkeys hanging from apron hooks."

"So you'll let me try out some of my recipes?" Hope sprang up in her.

"I'll give it some thought."

"For crying out loud, would it kill you to just say yes?"

He tapped his chin with a forefinger. "While you are an excellent chef, Melanie, I'm not convinced that letting you go wild with innovative preparations will bring in the business like you think it will. I believe the way to raise Chez Remy to the next level is to consistently serve top-notch, traditional meals."

"Traditional meals won't bring in hip and trendy clientele—the kind of clientele you need to make a splash."

"It's not about making a splash. It's about creating consistently superior food and service that people can rely on. A reputation is gained and maintained over time."

"What's wrong with making things happen now?"

"You're too impatient," he said.

"You're too cautious," she countered.

"Impulsiveness leads to disaster."

"Too much deliberation leads to missed opportunity."

"This city is rebuilding. People need something they can count on to stay the same. That's what Chez Remy is all about."

"That doesn't mean it can't change direction."

"There's nothing wrong with staying the course."

"You're just afraid," she challenged.

"Of what?"

"Of what we might stir up together."

"Are we talking about Chez Remy here? Or something else entirely?" His eyes locked with hers and she almost stopped breathing.

Melanie was vividly aware of everything. The feel of the concrete beneath her running shoes, the brilliant colors and intriguing smells of the market, the hungry taste of desire filling her mouth.

The same desire that was reflected in Robert's eyes.

He wanted her as much as she wanted him, but he was too prudent to act on those feelings.

"I'll tell you what I'm really afraid of when it comes to you and me partnering up," he murmured. "It's not your off-the-wall recipes or your passionate nature."

"What is it then?"

"You jump into things with enthusiasm, but I'm afraid you don't have the staying power for the long haul."

"Huh?"

"Frankly, Melanie, how can I go out on a limb with someone I can't trust to watch my back?"

THE WOUNDED EXPRESSION in Melanie's eyes told Robert he'd hurt her feelings.

Damn. That hadn't been his intention. He had no idea how to keep her both happy and at arm's length.

"Melanie...I—" He tried to apologize, but she wasn't listening.

She clamped her lips shut, blinked rapidly, then spun on her heel and disappeared into the crowd without another word.

See? That's what he was talking about. Whenever things got heated, Melanie walked away rather than hanging around to slog it out. But that didn't make him feel any better.

He hadn't been totally honest with her. Yes, he was afraid that if they teamed up to transform the restaurant, at some point she would leave him high and dry. But there was a lot more to his hesitation than that. He wasn't really worried about Chez Remy's. The restaurant had a solid reputation. What worried him was the way he felt whenever he was near her. Melanie made him want to do stupid, impulsive things. Like take her to bed.

Damn, but he wanted her.

And that did worry him.

He headed to his office at the hotel and tried to work on the upcoming menus for the celebration Chez Remy had planned for Mardi Gras, but he couldn't get Melanie out of his mind. She might appear to be tough and sassy, but he knew it was all an act designed to protect her heart. He had a few tricks like that of his own, and one of them was his journal.

He had just started writing her out of his system and onto the pages of his journal when the phone rang.

Caller ID told him the call was coming from the Stratosphere, his old place of employment in Seattle. He lifted the receiver with some trepidation. "Hello?"

"Robert, it's Joe Harding." Joe had taken over Robert's former job.

"Hey, Joe. What's up?" He tried to sound light and casual, but his grip on the phone tightened.

"Just thought you'd like to know someone's been calling around, asking questions about you."

"What kind of questions?"

"Personal questions."

"By someone, do you mean like the cops or a P.I.?"

"Don't know who he was, but he said he was asking for a friend down in New Orleans."

What was this all about? Were the Marchands checking his background? But why now, four months after they'd hired him? Robert's stomach tensed. Why couldn't the past stay buried, damn it? He'd paid for his mistakes.

"What did you tell the guy?" he asked Joe.

"Me? I said nothing, but some of the wait staff spoke to him. Don't know what they said."

"Thanks for letting me know. I appreciate it, Joe."

"Hey, I know you'd do the same for me."

Robert hung up the phone feeling unsettled. Who in New Orleans was having him investigated?

And why?

"ROBERT LESOEUR DOESN'T trust me to watch his back? Well, I don't trust him to watch mine." Melanie stormed into her apartment, mumbling under her breath and stripping off her sweaty exercise outfit as she went.

The little black kitten that had shown up on her doorstep last week darted under the couch. She'd fed it and now she didn't know what to do with it. She wasn't much of a pet person. Sweet as they were, pets tied you down. Realizing she'd startled the poor thing, she immediately softened her step and stopped grumbling.

"Here kitty, kitty, come see me." She dropped down on her knees and peered under the couch. The kitten eyed her with apprehension. She wriggled her fingers and the little creature came to her. "I'm sorry. We won't discuss Robert LeSoeur anymore."

Melanie cuddled the kitten for a few minutes, then set her down and headed for the bathroom. She tossed her clothes into the cheap discount store hamper someone had given her—why spend money on a fancy hamper when it just held dirty laundry?—then yanked the elastic band from her ponytail and tossed it onto the counter. She adjusted the shower as hot as she could stand it, stepped into the old claw-foot tub and pulled the curtain.

Steamy water trickled over her shoulders, calming her down. Okay, so maybe she'd overreacted to Robert's comment. Maybe she was just a little bit touchy on the subject. Maybe she hadn't always been the most responsible or reliable person in the world, but a girl could change. Problem was, how did you go about changing the mind of people who thought they had you pegged?

Sighing, she rested her forehead against the wall.

Face it, you have been unpredictable in the past. Who went backpacking through Europe after she dropped out of college, without thinking to inform her parents of that little detail until she was already in France, spending her tuition money on youth hostels and rail passes?

That was nine years ago and she'd paid her parents back.

Who got married three weeks to the day after David Muncie swept her off her feet, only to discover, six weeks into the marriage, that he was a control freak with an explosive temper and an addictive personality?

Remorsefully, Melanie rubbed a bar of honeysuckle-scented soap over the burn scar at the left side of her waist. But that was a long time ago, too. She hadn't done anything so rebellious or careless since then.

When she was away from New Orleans, people saw her as confident and capable. She kept her focus on her work and she was well-liked among her colleagues. In her old job, she'd been named employee of the month three times. And just before she'd left Boston to come home after her mother's heart attack, a headhunter had come snooping around, dangling visions of executive chef positions at five-star restaurants.

Melanie lathered her hair with shampoo and ruthlessly jammed her fingers through it, trying to scrub her regrets away. New Orleans might be where she was born, but it hadn't felt like home in a very long time.

How she wanted to belong here again! But was it even possible?

A forlorn loneliness seeped into her, and she stepped out of the tub, wrapped a thin towel around her wet hair and a thick fluffy bath towel around her body. The black kitten was curled up on the mat, eyes closed, purring like mad.

Well, at least someone trusted her.

Melanie reached down and scratched the kitten's soft fur, right behind her ears where she liked it. The happy purring intensified, and Melanie no longer felt so alone.

When had it started? This sense of separation from her family that often plagued her, even when she was in the same room with them?

It wasn't that her mother and father had teasingly called her their most wonderful little "oops." It had been no secret that Remy and Anne had thought their family was complete after Sylvie was born.

Her father had loved his four girls, but Melanie had always wondered if he'd secretly hoped for a son. At least she had been a tomboy, but it still hadn't been easy growing up the youngest. Her sisters had done everything ahead of her, and she never seemed able to catch up. But she still remembered exactly when it was that she realized how to get her family's attention.

The family had gone on the only vacation Melanie ever remembered them taking together. The hotel was closed for renovation, so her father had rented a camper and they'd driven to the Grand Canyon.

Melanie was six that summer. She and her sisters had ridden in the back of the camper, but after a while, she'd gotten claustrophobic. She'd had a panic attack and had to switch to the front seat, where she could see out to keep from becoming sick.

She'd loved that special time wedged between her parents, her sisters in the back. She'd pretended she was an only child. Remy had let her tune in the radio station of her choice, and she'd rested her head against Anne's shoulder, while her mother gently stroked her hair.

But once they arrived at the Grand Canyon, it was business

as usual. Her sisters came out of the camper and Melanie wasn't special anymore. She was the little one again, lost in the shuffle.

She'd had a temper tantrum at their picnic spot and her mother had made her go lie down in the back of the camper to cool off.

But Melanie had sneaked out when her mom wasn't looking, and hidden behind a pile of boulders to build a rock tower that would reach the moon.

Her tower didn't quite reach her waist, and looked more like a heap of rubble, but when she was finished, she'd hurried out to show her family what she'd done.

She could still see herself, crouching in the dirt, the Grand Canyon a panoramic background behind her, as she realized that the picnic table was empty, and the camper no longer parked alongside it.

Melanie let out a shriek and ran into the road just in time to see the camper disappearing around the bend.

They'd left her!

Her heart was pumping hard and she got that claustropho bic, carsick feeling all over again. Her family had driven away without her! They didn't want her anymore. She tasted the salt of her tears and put a fist to her stomach.

She'd felt so very, very small and all alone.

A hand clamped on her shoulder and she looked up, legs trembling, to see a kind-faced forest ranger in a Smokey the Bear hat staring down at her. "What are you doing out in the road, little girl?"

That's when she'd thrown up on him.

He'd taken her to the ranger's station, and a nice-smelling lady ranger had cleaned her up and then given her chocolate milk and cookies and a coloring book and crayons. Other grown-ups came to make a fuss over her, asking her name and where she was from. That's when she told them about her parents driving off and leaving her.

There was a flurry of activity and then some policemen showed up. Some time later another policeman came into the ranger station with her parents behind him.

Her mother scooped her into her arms and covered her face with kisses. Her sisters were crying and her father kept apologizing. Remy and Anne had thought she'd fallen asleep in the back of the camper with the other girls, and her sisters had thought she was in the front with their parents. It wasn't until the state trooper pulled them over to tell them they'd left a daughter behind that they had even known she was missing.

Her mother kept a tight grip on Melanie for the rest of the day. Her sisters sang her songs and told her stories. Her father let her pick the restaurant for their evening meal. Everyone paid her lot of attention, and it was glorious.

And that's when the realization hit her. If you wanted to get noticed, you had to rock the boat.

So began Melanie's flirtation with rebellion. Whenever she felt ignored or left out, she would do something outrageous to make them remember that she was there.

She'd turned into a naughty girl.

But she was a girl no more. She was a grown woman who was determined to make up for her past mistakes and prove to everyone that they could indeed depend on her.

Robert LeSoeur included.

CHAPTER FOUR

AFTER HER QUICK SHOWER and a change of clothes, Melanie met her sisters for Saturday morning brunch at La Grand-mère's. As they waited in line for the maître d', Melanie glanced at her oldest sister.

How lovely Charlotte was, with sleek hair the color of toasted pecans and exotic, almond-shaped green eyes. She possessed a timeless beauty, a genteel Southern charm she'd picked up from their mother. She had a sense of grace that Melanie had never learned—never cared to learn, actually.

Charlotte smiled at the middle-aged maître d', laid two polished fingertips against the back of his hand and sweetly asked for the best table they had with a view of the Mississippi. They were seated immediately at a corner table overlooking the river.

No doubt, Char had a way about her. She was all cream and roses. All pearls and lace. She still wore stockings, even during the muggy New Orleans summer months. Next to her elegant oldest sister, Melanie felt shabby, eclipsed, invisible.

Renee sat on Melanie's right. A couple of years younger than Charlotte, the former Hollywood studio executive was now in charge of hotel public relations, and she looked the part. Renee was willow thin and kept her pale blond hair styled in a simple but chic shoulder-length cut. There was no denying the glow in her sister's eyes since she and Pete Traynor had fallen in love.

Melanie tried to shrug off a twinge of jealousy. She wasn't normally the envious type. What was wrong with her today?

"No beignets for me," Renee said when the waiter brought a complimentary basket of the square French doughnuts, deep fried and dusted with powered sugar, to the table. "I've been overindulging lately."

"Great." Melanie reached for the basket. "More for me."

"You're so lucky," Charlotte said. "You've never had to worry about your weight."

"That's because Mel's always in motion," said Sylvie, the sister closest to Melanie in age. "She burns off the calories before they have a chance to stick to her hips."

"As if you have anything to complain about." Melanie licked powdered sugar off her fingers with a groan of appreciation. "I'd kill for curves like yours."

Sylvie was the quintessential Bohemian earth mother with her curly red hair, green eyes, fair skin and heart-shaped face. She was also plainspoken, and her honesty took some people off guard. She had moved home to run the art gallery at the hotel, bringing her daughter with her. Daisy Rose was now an adorable three-year-old and Anne's only grandchild to date. The entire family spoiled her shamelessly.

Her sisters were all so different from her, Melanie thought, even physically. She was the only one who'd inherited their father's dark coloring.

Like Renee, Sylvie had just recently fallen madly in love. Her beau, Jefferson Lambert, was a widowed New England lawyer with a teenage daughter, and he and Sylvie took turns shuttling between Boston and New Orleans.

It seemed love was in the air at the Hotel Marchand.

For everybody except me.

Not that Melanie wanted to get married again. She'd had enough of that nonsense, thank you very much. But she wouldn't mind having a boyfriend.

Of course, she hadn't included Charlotte.

Melanie cast a glance at her sister and wondered if Charlotte had given up on love entirely. At forty, she looked a good five years younger, but Charlotte lived and breathed the family business to the exclusion of a personal life. Like Melanie, she'd been married before and divorced.

Odd to think they had something in common. They were so dissimilar in every other way, from their height to their dispositions.

"I know I shouldn't." Sylvie winked conspiratorially at Melanie. "But pass the beignets."

She grinned and handed the basket of deep-fried dough to her sister. As a kid, Melanie had easily coaxed Sylvie into going along with her schemes, even though Sylvie was the one who usually got into trouble because she was six years older and should have known better. But Sylvie inevitably forgave her.

"What are the rest of you doing with all those childhood mementos Mother's been giving you?" Renee asked. "I'm running out of storage space."

"I just shoved them in a closet." Sylvie dabbed powered sugar off her chin.

"I've got mine in storage," Charlotte said. "There's no room in my house. You can toss your things in with mine if you want, Renee."

"What old childhood junk?" A tiny stab of the same aban-
donment she'd felt the day she watched the camper disappear
around the bend at the Grand Canyon prodded Melanie.

"Mère's on a cleaning spurt," Charlotte explained. "I think
she's getting restless, and since we're doing our best to keep
her from coming back full time to the hotel, she's looking for
things to do."

"She hasn't given me any childhood keepsakes."

"She probably hasn't unearthed yours yet," Renee said.
"Don't worry, you'll get them, and then you'll wish you
hadn't, because you won't know what to do with them."

Unless Mother didn't keep any of my stuff. Melanie shook
off the thought.

"So, Char," she said, after the waiter had brought them all
chicory coffee and taken their breakfast orders. Her sister
didn't like having her name shortened, but Melanie did it just
to tease her. She was the only one who could get away with
it. "What's this tête-à-tête about?"

Charlotte fingered the strand of pearls at her neck. "The
Charboneaux-Long wedding is next Saturday and I'm cir-
cling the wagons. Considering the problems we've had lately,
I'm planning to bring in additional security.

"This wedding is the event of the social season, and the last
thing we want is for anything to mar Carly Charboneaux's big
day. I need all of you to make sure the event runs flawlessly.
After that incident with Ella Emerson, we have to make sure
we keep the press at bay. If you notice anything out of the
ordinary, let me know no matter how inconsequential it seems."

Melanie thought of Robert and the reporter. Should she
say something or keep quiet?

Restlessly, her mind wandered, recalling what had

happened in the kitchen yesterday afternoon and in the market this morning. She thought of Robert's long muscular frame. The way he carried himself, slightly aloof, but with the confidence of a man accustomed to being in tight control of his feelings. She imagined running her fingers through his thatch of thick, wavy, wheat colored hair and rumpling it sexily across his forehead.

Whenever she thought about him, her body throbbed, and suddenly she felt hot and edgy.

"Botching the Carboneaux wedding would be a PR nightmare." Renee's words pulled Melanie from her reverie. "I'm not sure how I could get us out of that one."

The waiter delivered their breakfast, and Melanie waited to speak until he was out of earshot.

"Is there anything I can do to take some of the burden off your shoulders? I want to help. Put me to work."

Charlotte raised a perfectly arched eyebrow. "Is this a serious offer?"

"Of course."

"Well, if you really mean it, then yes, there's something you can do."

"Name it."

"Could you take my place at Grand-mère's charity auction on Thursday night? I'm completely swamped and I honestly didn't know how I was going to manage to fit it in. It'd be a godsend if you could step in."

Melanie clamped her teeth tightly together to keep from groaning aloud. This wasn't what she'd had in mind when she'd offered to help. Getting involved with their grandmother Celeste's pet projects was never her idea of a good time, and being the youngest, she rarely got tapped to pitch in. But there was no backing out now. Not when she was trying to prove to her family that she could be depended upon.

"Um…is this the bachelorette auction?"

"Yes."

Great. She couldn't think of anything more humiliating than being put up for auction so that well-heeled, middle-aged fat cats could drool over her. "Er…I suppose so."

"No supposing," Charlotte said. "This event is very important to Grand-mère. It's either yes or no."

"Yes, okay. I'll do it."

"You won't back out at the last minute?"

"What do you take me for? A quitter?"

Charlotte, Renee and Sylvie exchanged looks.

"I never said you were a quitter," Charlotte protested.

"Then why did you even ask the question?" Here she was, back at home, cast in the unreliable-baby-sister role again.

"Well," Charlotte said, "I know you're professional when it comes to your work at the restaurant, but you do have trouble keeping other commitments, and if you don't show up, Grand-mère will blame me. Like she did when you were supposed to drive her to her doctor's appointment, but took off to go to a keg party with your boyfriend."

"That was ten years ago!"

"I'm just saying…"

"I'll be there." Melanie gritted her teeth.

"All right then. I'll bring the dress over to your apartment on Monday. It might have to be adjusted." Charlotte looked as if she might say something else, but then just pressed her lips together, nodded and sent Melanie a look that said, *I'm giving you a chance to prove me wrong.*

Fine. That's all she needed. A chance.

She would not let her sister down this time.

MELANIE WAS THE FIRST to leave the restaurant after brunch was over.

As Charlotte watched her walk away, saucy black ponytail swishing in time to her long-legged trot, a knot of concern formed in her stomach. She and Melanie had often butted heads over the years, whenever Charlotte stepped into a surrogate mother role, but there was a special love in her heart for her youngest sister. Something was disturbing Melanie, but she had no idea what it was. Her baby sister had been distracted almost the entire time they'd been together.

"Do you think that Melanie is going to stay in New Orleans this time?" Charlotte asked her other sisters.

Sylvie shrugged. "She's been back for four months and that's the longest time she's stayed since she left home, but when it comes to Melanie, who can say for sure what she'll do?"

"Exactly. I'm worried that she's ready for a change. She seems edgy lately. Restless."

"I hadn't noticed anything out of the ordinary," Renee said. "Except that she doesn't seem to be getting along with Robert."

"What do you mean?" That bit of news definitely left Charlotte feeling uneasy. If Melanie was having problems at work, Charlotte might have to intervene for professional reasons.

"It's just kitchen gossip. Hearsay."

"Let me know if you find out anything I should be worried about." Charlotte once again toyed with the strand of pearls at her neck.

"Our Melanie is a restless soul," Sylvie said. "She's not the kind of person who sticks in one place for long."

"I wish she would stay." Charlotte sighed. "Chez Remy's

been a different place since she came home. The kitchen is alive again, the way it was when Papa was here. Plus, I worry about her when she's out in the world alone with no family nearby."

"Maybe you should tell her that," Sylvie suggested.

"I would except I don't want to influence her to stay if that's not what she really wants."

"Maybe her footloose phase is over. She will be turning thirty soon," Renee added.

Charlotte had never had the luxury of a "footloose phase" and she didn't understand her sister's restless nature. Remy and Anne had been consumed with getting the Hotel Marchand up and running during Charlotte's childhood and teenage years, and they'd relied on her help in raising her younger siblings. Not that she'd minded. Caring for those girls, Melanie in particular, since she was so much younger, had been the joy of Charlotte's life. She'd gone into the family business, but secretly harbored a little resentment that none of her sisters had followed in her footsteps. They didn't seem to realize the sacrifices she'd made for the family.

But Charlotte wasn't one to martyr herself. She'd chosen this path. She could have veered off if she'd wanted to. She didn't blame anyone, and nothing meant more to her than her family and the Hotel Marchand.

Sylvie reached out and laid a hand over Charlotte's. "Whatever happens, we'll be okay. We've survived a lot these last few years and our bond has only grown stronger."

To an extent, that was true. First their father's death, then Hurricane Katrina, and recently their mother's heart attack. It was Anne's illness that had brought Renee and Melanie back to New Orleans. But Charlotte couldn't help feeling that

Melanie was conflicted about staying. She wished she knew what was bothering her sister deep down inside.

"Try not to fret too much about Mel," Sylvie said. "She's resilient as rubber. Remember that time Mama and Papa pulled a *Home Alone* and left Melanie behind at the Grand Canyon? When the state trooper took us to her, she was sitting like a princess, surrounded by her admirers, drinking chocolate milk and eating cookies and coloring in a Barbie coloring book with a sixty-four pack of crayons. I was so jealous."

Charlotte shuddered. "I don't remember it that way at all. I remember her looking sad and lost and lonely in spite of the attention and the cookies and the coloring book. I remember feeling so guilty because I should have been watching her. It was my fault we left her behind."

"You've always taken on too much responsibility for things that were beyond your control," Renee chided her. "Come on, you were what? Sixteen?"

"Sixteen going on sixty," Sylvie added. "Renee's right. Stop assuming responsibility for everyone else's happiness. You've got enough things on your plate as it is. Don't worry about Mel until you find out there's something to worry about."

Charlotte nodded. Her sisters were right. But even though she tried to put it from her mind, she couldn't help feeling that there was something going on in Melanie's life, and her baby sister was just too proud to ask for their advice.

BACK AT CHEZ REMY, Melanie stood at the stove stirring diablo sauce for the red grouper starring on the Saturday night dinner menu. She cast a sidelong glance at Robert, who'd just strolled into the kitchen.

"I had a dream last night," she said.

"About me?" He flashed her his dimples.

Yes. "No, don't be silly. Why would I dream about you? I dreamed of a great new recipe."

"I'm disappointed," he said. "I thought maybe you'd dreamed about me."

"Get over yourself. I dream about food."

"That's it? Nothing about me?"

Melanie tried not to be charmed. "Are you going to let me try out the recipe? Or do I have to mention to Charlotte that I saw you talking to the *Times-Picayune* reporter?"

Robert skewered her with his gaze, but a smile twitched at his lips. "Are you threatening me?"

"*Threaten* is such an ugly word. I prefer to think of it as negotiation."

"I've got nothing to hide. Blackmail away."

"Nothing?" She arched an eyebrow. "No deep dark secrets rattling around in your closet?"

It wasn't her imagination. A quick but unmistakable guilty expression flashed across his features. Maybe he did have something to hide.

"Tell me about the recipe," he said.

"A Valentine's specialty, although I'm thinking it could be great for Mardi Gras as well."

His eyes narrowed. "What have you got in mind?"

"Oysters," she said.

"Why am I not surprised?"

"Succulent, wet, slippery." The words were like an invitation. "Served with a champagne mignonette sauce."

"Sexy," he said.

"That's the point. But I'm not done yet."

"What else?"

"On a bed of tender, yet still firm, sautéed asparagus spears."

Melanie could practically see Robert's mind traveling the track she'd set up.

"And get this," she murmured. "The whole thing is topped by white truffles dripping with hot, melted butter."

A sexy glint in his eye, he lowered his head and whispered so only she could hear. "You're very wicked."

The kitchen was crowded. Staff members bustled to and fro. The lack of privacy should have been embarrassing. Instead, it was strangely erotic.

Their gazes fused.

A shock of sexual awareness, so overwhelmingly strong it stole her breath, jolted through Melanie. She took a step backward. The curve of her spine bumped into the counter as she willed herself not to blush.

"Something's burning."

"Huh?" Her body was on full alert but her brain felt sluggish and she couldn't process what Robert had just said.

He nodded toward the stove. An acrid smell filled the air.

Her diablo sauce!

In her hormone-induced trance, she'd stopped stirring, and the sauce was scorching on the bottom of the pan.

Mindlessly, she grabbed for the saucepan to pull it off the burner, but her elbow struck the handle and sent it flying. The pan clattered to the floor, splashing hot pottage on her bare ankles and shins. Of all the days to wear a skirt.

"Oww," she howled, hopping from one stinging leg to the other.

In an instant, Robert had hold of her.

Melanie had no idea what he intended. She was too busy

hissing with pain. He bent and scooped her into his arms, peeling off her kitchen clogs with his broad hand.

She squeezed her eyes tightly shut against the burning sensation. Robert tucked her butt solidly in the curve of his left arm, stood up and rushed her across the room to the sink. He dangled her legs over the stainless steel basin and carefully hosed the sauce off with the vegetable sprayer.

The cool water brought immediate relief.

She let her head sag against his shoulder. She weighed a hundred thirty-six pounds, and Robert was holding her with the same ease she held her niece, Daisy Rose. Behind her, she heard someone pick up the saucepan from the floor and begin cleaning up the spill.

"I'll get that," she said. "It's my mess."

"Hush," Robert commanded, but in a tender way.

Melanie hushed.

He wrapped clean dish towels around her burns and carried her toward his office.

"I can walk," she protested.

"I know that."

"So put me down."

"Not yet."

"You'll hurt your back."

"I'll take my chances."

"Stubborn man."

"Smart-mouthed woman."

He paraded her through the kitchen, past the curious stares of the other cooks.

"I'm sorry for the mess," she declared as Robert waltzed her past the busboy, who was busily wiping Diablo sauce off the front of the stove.

Smiling shyly, Raoul made brief eye contact before quickly ducking his head and intensifying his scrubbing.

"Gosh," Melanie murmured under her breath, awareness dawning. "I never realized it before, but I think the kid might have a crush on me."

"Are you blind? The entire kitchen staff has a crush on you." Robert's voice was gruff.

"Really?"

She glanced around the room and realized every eye in the place was on her. Just because they were staring at her didn't mean they had a crush on her. Although come to think about it, the guys did stare at her a lot.

"As if you didn't know."

Honestly, she didn't know. Was he right?

"Allison, too?" she teased, more to keep her mind off the feel of Robert's arms around her than the sting of the burns. She was referring to Chez Remy's assistant pastry chef.

"No, not Allison, but everyone else." Robert backed into his office, pushing the door open with his shoulder, Melanie still clutched in his arms.

You included? Melanie wanted to ask, but she was afraid of how he might answer. What if he said yes?

She was feeling a little whacked out from the conflicting emotions surging through her and the stinging pain in her legs. Her belly burned and her pulse fluttered wildly at the hollow of her throat.

Inside his office, Robert eased her into the chair parked behind the teakwood desk that had been in her family for over a hundred years. The top of the desk was spit-and-polish tidy. Papers were stacked neatly in either the in-box or the outgoing file. The nearby bookcase was filled with cookbooks, nutrition texts and business tomes. Even the trash can had recently been emptied.

Robert's masculine fragrance clung to the chair's gray tweed fabric. The rich woodsy scent teased her olfactory receptors, as if whispering, *This is for you.*

Melanie wasn't one to ignore her instincts. No matter what her head was telling her about Robert—that he was all wrong for her—her body's chemistry was singing a very different tune.

He knelt on the hand-woven rug in front of her and cupped her right heel in his palm. The expression in his eyes was so exquisitely tender she couldn't bear to look.

"It's my fault you burned your legs," he said. "I distracted you while you were working."

"Oh, please." She waved a hand. "Don't tell me you're one of those people."

"What people?"

"The kind who want to assume responsibility for everything that happens. Like my sister Charlotte. It's not your fault that I had my head up my…" She stopped herself just in time before using the earthy language that had gotten her in a lot of trouble when she was a kid. "…in the clouds."

"It's my kitchen. I'm in charge."

"You're not God," she said. "Accidents happen."

"You know," he mused, his fingers tenderly holding her foot, "there's a philosophy that says there are no accidents."

"What? You're saying I dropped a pan of diablo sauce and burned my legs just to get you to take me into your office so I could be alone with you?"

"Did you?" He cocked his head.

"I'm not that calculating, LeSoeur. In case you haven't noticed, I shoot from the hip."

"And ask questions later," he muttered.

She suddenly wanted to yank her foot away, but instead sank her top teeth into her bottom lip. Not to brace herself against the pain, but against the unexpected pleasure of his touch. She felt unsettled in a strange and unaccustomed way.

When his fingers gently crept up her leg to remove the towels he'd wrapped around her burns, Melanie realized the man was a lot more sensual than she'd given him credit for. His caress was lighter than oxygen and way too thrilling.

"Slide out that bottom drawer." Robert gestured with his head, inclining it toward the desk drawer at her right. "There's a first-aid kit inside."

She leaned over the arm of the chair, grabbed the drawer handle, tugged it open and found the kit.

He took it from her with his free hand.

Their fingers brushed and she felt a wildfire of sensation. He pretended to be absorbed with opening the box and taking out a jar of cream to rub on her burns.

"More than likely it's only first degree," he noted, swabbing her legs with the soothing salve and then taping nonstick Telfa gauze over the wounds. "Probably won't even blister."

"That's good," she said, her voice sounding faraway and kind of fuzzy, even to her own ears. The way his fingers tickled her flesh made her insides tremble like an addict in need of a fix.

He angled his head and stared at her with sultry eyes. Although he pressed his lips tightly together, she could see what he was trying so desperately to hide.

Stark, hungry need.

Melanie looked into his eyes, ached to feel the pressure of his lips against hers. She couldn't keep resisting her impulses. It went against her nature. So without fully considering what she was about to do, she leaned forward, puckered her lips and prayed he would take the hint.

CHAPTER FIVE

DAMN HIM, HE SHOULD not have kissed her.

But he had.

Robert was weak from four months of fighting the attraction. He was just a guy, with a caveman desire for the luscious woman in front of him. He couldn't think about anything except how much he wanted her. He was ready to wave the white flag. He was going to have to do a hell of a lot of journal writing to tame this beast.

He blamed their close proximity, the privacy of his office, the hot diablo sauce and the fact that her delicate foot was cushioned in his palm. He faulted the devilish glint in her indigo eyes as she leaned forward, revealing an exquisite view of her cleavage and just daring him to kiss her. He laid blame on the sweet, full, puckered lips hovering mere inches from his own. But most of all, Robert held himself responsible. He'd been too long without sex, his judgment seriously clouded by testosterone, or he would have remembered that this was Melanie Marchand, his boss's sister. If anything went wrong between them, he'd be the one to lose his job, not her.

Her lips parted, and the sight of that impish pink tongue was his total undoing. Her eyes were locked on his, the muscles in her throat moving as she swallowed.

He was careening toward a head-on collision with professional disaster and he knew it, but in the heat of the moment he simply didn't care. His mind was that skewed by her. Robert reached up and pulled the elastic band from her ponytail. Her hair fell over his hand in a shiny dark cascade.

Sharply, he inhaled.

Her eyes widened.

He sank his lips onto hers.

She let out a soft sound of pleasure and arched against him. Underneath her shirt, he felt her nipples pebble. She smelled so good, like the Cajun holy trinity of bell peppers, celery and onions.

He cupped her face in his palm, amazed at her softness. Her hair was tangled around his fingers, ribbons of ebony silk.

With a sigh, she wound her arms around his neck, pulling him deeper into the kiss.

A scorching heat flashed through him, incinerating everything in its path. His tongue, his throat, his gut.

He was on fire for her.

The taste of her mouth. Wow!

Kissing her was raw and real, primal and fierce.

Perfectly, their mouths fit together. The scrape of his skin—already sprouting a slight stubble even though he'd shaved that morning—against her tender chin made for an intoxicating contrast. She was all woman and he was all man.

Naked need, passionate frustration, pure animal lust erupted and spun a magic that went far beyond the mere joining of their lips. This single, wild union was everything.

Robert fisted his hand tighter in her hair and pulled her even closer to him, penetrating her with his tongue, exploring her fully. Ah yes, yes. This was what he'd been tasting in his dreams.

He groaned low in his throat, his body straining and pushing against hers, and Melanie met him measure for measure—a sensual woman unabashed in her sexuality.

His lips vibrated against hers as he breathed, "Melanie."

No name had never sounded so sexy.

She moaned quietly and he swallowed up the resonant sound, like a man too long deprived of what every cell in his body cried out for.

He yearned to tumble her onto a soft mattress, rip her clothes off and dive into her. He ached to feel her body close around his.

He was in turmoil, excitement warring with caution. And guilt.

He jerked his head back, yanking away, struggling to snatch hold of some shred of sanity before it was too late. Her eyes were clouded and heavy-lidded. Her lips trembling...

He wasn't the only one totally blown away. Embarrassment and regret washed over him.

"Melanie..." What was he going to say? That he was sorry? But he wasn't sorry. He'd enjoyed every minute of it.

She reached out to draw him back to her, but he raised an arm, blocking her hand. He was breathing hard and he couldn't speak, but he flashed her a desperate message with his eyes.

Touch me again and I will have no choice but to take you right here, right now, the rest of the world be damned.

At that moment a knock sounded, and they had just enough time to jump apart before the door swung open and Jean-Paul stuck his head into the room. "Kitchen's gone crazy busy, Chef LeSoeur. We're really in the weeds. Is Mel okay to come back to work?"

IT WAS AFTER MIDNIGHT when Melanie left the restaurant. She floated, flying high on the long-acting endorphin rush of Robert's kiss.

She'd imagined that he'd be a terrific kisser, strong and masterful. But there was also a surprisingly tender side to him she hadn't expected. She'd felt it in the gentle sweep of his tongue as he'd explored her mouth. She wondered how far things might have gone if Jean-Paul hadn't interrupted at just the wrong time. Or maybe it had been the right time. His interruption had kept her from making a huge mistake.

Car keys in hand, she stepped out into the courtyard and was surprised to find Charlotte sitting on one of the wrought-iron benches in the patio garden. The pool area glistened in the muted lighting. Overhead the stars were rich and bright against an inky sky. Her sister was a meadowlark who rarely stayed up past ten. Why was she still at the hotel?

"Char?" Melanie ambled over.

Charlotte looked up, her face wan in the moonlight. "Hello, Melanie."

"What are you doing out here all by your lonesome? Why don't you go on home?"

"I can't turn my mind off with everything that's going on right now."

The cool February night breeze gusted, and Charlotte pulled her sweater tighter around her shoulders. There was a strain around her mouth that concerned Melanie.

"You want me to make you some warm milk?" She gestured toward the kitchen. "Might help you sleep."

"No thanks, I'm fine. I'll go home in a minute."

"You don't look fine. You look exhausted."

"I am a bit. I think everything's finally starting to catch up with me—Mom's heart attack, the problems we've had recently at the hotel. I'm not as young I used to be."

"You're not old." Melanie plunked down beside her. It wasn't like her competent, efficient older sister to admit a weakness, and she felt honored that Charlotte would confide in her. "Want to talk about what's on your mind?"

Charlotte gave a humorless laugh. "I'm supposed to be the one getting you to talk, not the other way around."

"Talk? What do you want me to talk about?"

"Why you've been so on edge lately. Moody. You're normally a pretty upbeat person, Melanie."

"I haven't been moody," she said automatically, then realized she had and it was all due to this infernal attraction to Robert that she had no idea how to handle.

"You seem distracted. Like you've got a lot on your mind." Charlotte paused and studied her for a long moment. "Is there something you need to tell me?"

Melanie tugged the elastic band from her ponytail, wrapped it around her wrist and fluffed her hair with her fingers. It had been a madhouse in the kitchen tonight. Robert had pitched in during the worst of the dinner rush, working side by side with her at the stove to prepare a new batch of diablo sauce, but instead of being helpful, as he'd intended, he was a major distraction.

She hadn't been able to stop sending him sidelong glances.

Or noticing how good he smelled. Like food and hard work and treacherous man.

Yeah, she wanted to say. *Robert LeSoeur is driving me crazy and I don't know what to do about it. Fire the guy and*

I'll be fine. Instead she said, "How come you and Mom never considered offering me the executive chef position?"

Melanie hadn't asked the question that had been eating at her for four months because her feelings had been hurt and she'd been too busy pretending that she didn't care. But this seemed like the right time to bring it up. She would tell her.

"We considered it."

"And you decided to hire an outsider over family. Why? You don't think I'm capable of running Chez Remy?"

"It's not that at all."

"What is it then?"

Charlotte interlaced her fingers and brought them up to press flat against her lips. Melanie recognized the sign. Her sister was trying to think of how best to phrase her statement.

For some reason, the gesture irritated her. Charlotte was so damn controlled she even rehearsed her words before she let them out of her mouth.

"Egads, Charlotte, just come right out and say what's on your mind."

Her sister looked startled. "I was just…"

"I know what you were just doing. You were carefully considering every word. For crying out loud, be spontaneous for once in your life."

"That's what you want?"

"Yes."

"Okay, fine. Mother and I felt the job was too administrative for you. You're creative and you would feel stifled within a matter of weeks."

"You're saying I'm too irresponsible for the job?"

"I didn't say that."

"It's what you were thinking."

Leave it alone, a voice in the back of Melanie's head warned. *You won't feel any better when Charlotte confirms what you already believe.*

"Mom and I thought if you had the executive chef position, you'd start resenting the responsibility, grow restless and end up leaving sooner than if we hadn't given you the job. But the truth is, we didn't think you'd want the position. Come on, Mel, if you really wanted to stay here you wouldn't still be subletting your apartment in Boston."

Melanie opened her mouth to refute the argument, but realized her sister had a point. She was still holding on to her Boston apartment, keeping her options open. She did chafe whenever she felt her choices narrowing. But it hurt to think her family didn't believe she could step up to the plate and pinch-hit when they needed her.

"You want someone you can depend on as executive chef, and I'm just not dependable, is that it?"

"Be fair," Charlotte said. "You haven't exactly been the poster child for steady and stable. You went to how many colleges before you dropped out to go to culinary school?"

"Five, but that's only because Mama and Papa wanted me to go to university. All I ever wanted to do was cook. Besides, you're supposed to be confused and reckless when you're in college."

"I wasn't."

"Of course not," Melanie said. "You're Saint Charlotte, who never does anything wrong."

"Look," Charlotte said, ignoring her comment in that saintlike way of hers. "You've moved from job to job and guy to guy. You married David on the spur of the moment and divorced him just as quickly. You can't balance your checkbook. You don't have a dime in savings. And you're always off on one travel adventure or the other."

She paused and took a deep breath before continuing. "Which is all fine—it's your life, your prerogative. But the Hotel Marchand is my life. I love you, Melanie, but I needed someone I could rely on. Someone like Robert. You want me to be blunt? Well, here's me being blunt. We didn't offer you the position because we knew we couldn't count on you."

The honesty she'd begged for was devastating.

To hear that her sister actually thought such things about her shattered Melanie's heart.

She wanted to burst into tears, but she forced them back. She'd asked for the truth, and ugly as it was, her sister had given it to her.

Melanie swallowed hard, choking back her sadness. "Felt kinda good, though, didn't it? Speaking your mind." She gave Charlotte a half grin, struggling not to reveal her pain, using the old a-good-offense-is-the-best-defense ploy.

"This is how you get into trouble, letting your thoughts flow uncensored from your mouth."

"And overthinking things is the reason you're stuck in a life you don't really want," Melanie challenged.

Charlotte gasped. "I love my life."

"Do you?" Melanie arched her eyebrows. "Really? Or are you so into being the good girl and doing what's expected of you that you've never even examined what it is that you really want?"

He sister said nothing, but she was breathing heavily, struggling to tamp down her anger, rein in her control.

"Char…Charlotte."

Melanie felt contrite. She was so sorry she'd lashed out. Her sister meant well. Their approach to life was very different, that was all. She had no business saying what she'd just said.

"I'm so sorry," she exclaimed. "I meant to cheer you up, to make you feel better, not start a fight."

"I'm sorry, too." Charlotte held out her arms. "Give me a hug?"

Melanie melted into her older sister's embrace and they hugged each other tightly. "I'm going to try really hard to be a better person. I promise."

"Honey, just be yourself."

"I have been, but lately it feels like I've outgrown the old me."

Charlotte laughed. "You're just looking down the barrel of the big three-O. Turning thirty makes you reevaluate everything."

"Tell me about it." Melanie chuckled ruefully.

"If there's ever anything you need to talk about, I want you to know that I'm here for you."

"Thank you for saying so."

"I'm glad we got this out in the open. I think I can get some sleep now."

"Me, too." They smiled at each other, and love for her sister filled the lonely spot in Melanie's heart. "And Char?"

"Yes?"

"If for some reason Robert decides to quit, could I be considered for the executive chef job?"

"Sure, of course. If you really wanted it, but I don't think Robert's going anywhere. I heard him telling Luc he was buying a house here."

"Really?" Melanie's hopes sank.

She felt so conflicted. On the one hand she would love to be the executive chef of Chez Remy, but as Charlotte had pointed out, it was a big commitment. Running a restaurant involved managerial skills and Robert seemed perfect for the job.

So where did that leave her in the grand scheme of things?

WHEN MELANIE ARRIVED at work the next day she received an unexpected surprise. Her chocolate turkey was featured as the evening special. A gleeful sense of victory swept over her and she rode the feeling like a prize-winning racehorse.

Robert had caved.

"I should have burned my legs ages ago," she muttered to herself. "Or kissed him."

"Pardon?" Jean-Paul asked.

"What's up with the chocolate turkey?"

The Cajun winked. "I thought you two negotiated a peace treaty last night."

"Not hardly." She didn't want the staff to be aware of the change in her relationship with Robert. As far as they were concerned he was still her adversary.

"Well, whatever went on back there in the boss's office last night, looks like you won."

"Nothing went on."

"Maybe you don't think so, but something must have changed. You got your way and Chef LeSoeur, he don't give in so easy."

That was true.

Hmm, what *was* up?

Pensively, she tied on her apron. She heard the sound of Robert's crocodile shoes creaking softly against the floor. Even without the noisy shoes, she would have recognized his walk if she were blindfolded in a crowd. There was a methodical crispness to his gait. A certainty that said he never made a misstep.

And now she knew that, unlike her arrogant ex-husband, Robert was capable of compromise. He'd put chocolate turkey on the menu. He was going to let her take a chance, with *his* reputation on the line. It was something David would never have done. Once her ex made a decision, he never went back on it, even in the face of flagrant proof that he was wrong. Unless, that is, he was conniving to get something in return.

Was that what Robert was doing? Did he want something from her in exchange? Did he have an ulterior motive?

Now that was a thought.

Melanie turned to find Robert standing directly behind her. She startled, seeing him so close.

He looked at her and she looked at him, and everything felt crazy, weird and dangerous.

"What's this all about?" She gestured at the menu board. "You're okaying the chocolate turkey?"

"It's only a test drive," he said. "If it doesn't sell, it's out of here."

"But why did you give in?"

"I gave it some thought and decided that you had a valid point. Your chocolate turkey deserved a chance. The customers should decide the fate of a dish, not me."

Damn. Why had he gone and done a nice thing like that? Now she was nervous, worried the dish would be a smashing flop. "But why the change of heart?"

He shrugged.

"I know what this is about." Melanie glanced over her shoulder at the kitchen help, then stepped closer to Robert and lowered her voice. "This is about last night."

"Excuse me?" His voice was as low as hers. He flicked a

lazy glance over her body, and a thoroughly masculine smirk lifted the corners of his mouth.

"You're feeling guilty for having taken advantage of me in a moment of vulnerability," she teased.

"Yes," he said. "I do feel guilty. But that's not why I put the turkey on the menu."

Around them came the sounds of chopping and peeling and slicing and dicing. The food processor whirled. The radio perched on the windowsill played zydeco music. The air was thick with steam from the kettle of gumbo simmering on the back stove, the perfect blend of garlic and onions and bell peppers scenting the air.

As Melanie stared into Robert's eyes, the background sounds and smells faded away and all she could think was *I'm in deep trouble here*.

And then she saw something in his face that surprised her, something that took her thoughts from herself and her own concerns. Robert looked like a man who'd been hurt deeply and was scared of finding himself right back at a place he thought he'd left far behind. There was a melancholia about him that she'd only caught quick glimpses of before.

A loneliness, a longing. She understood how that felt, and it called to something familiar inside of her.

She kept staring at him, trying to see more, read him better, but his expression changed and he put a sexy smile on his face, belying the darkness lurking in his eyes just seconds earlier.

Had she imagined it?

"How's the burn?"

She glanced down. She'd taken off the bandage. The burn was nothing but faint pink streaks now. "Feeling no pain, thanks to your quick response and first aid."

"I'm glad."

More awkward silence stretched between them. This time he was the one who rushed to fill it.

"Your turkey awaits." He gestured toward the bird laid out on the prep table.

"Are you trying to butter me up for some reason?" she asked, still feeling suspicious, waiting for the other shoe to drop. He was being too nice. What was the catch?

"Guilty," he admitted.

She should have known. A guy who could admit he was wrong, with no strings attached, was a mythological creature.

Melanie crossed her arms over her chest. "What is it?"

"You've got to make me a promise."

"I don't make promises until I know what it is I'm promising," she said.

"We can't have a repeat of last night."

"You're saying no more kissing?"

"Precisely."

"Why not?" On the one hand, she agreed with him completely, but on the other hand, she really wanted to kiss him again. Fool that she was.

"We need to set a good example for the rest of the kitchen staff."

"Lame. I'm not buying it."

"It would disrupt our work environment."

He had a point. She thought of how her volatile relationship with her ex had boiled over on the job.

"Especially," Robert continued, "when things don't work out between us."

"What makes you think things couldn't work out?" she asked.

His expression grew serious. "Come on, Melanie, we're night and day. The best we could hope for would be a lot of great sex."

"And what's wrong with that?"

"No matter how hard you try to keep emotions out of it, sex always complicates things."

"You don't know what you're missing," she teased.

Robert's smile was wistful. "I'm certain you're right about that."

"Be honest. You're afraid of me, aren't you? That's the real reason."

"Hell, yes."

"How come?"

"You're way more woman than I can handle." His gaze traveled from her eyes to her lips and lower.

"Is that a compliment or a complaint?"

"I like things ordered, organized, predictable."

"I know that. The first thing you did when you got this job was label the shelves and have everyone's name sewn on their aprons. But here's a little secret." She leaned closer, her lips grazing his ear. "Predictable is boring."

She didn't imagine it; he was doing his best not to shudder. Oh yeah. Whether he knew it or not, she could have him if she wanted him. Question was, did she want him?

"Predictable is safe," he continued.

"What's so great about safety?"

"Cuts down on the chaos."

"What's wrong with chaos?"

"It's messy."

"What's wrong with messy?"

"It's out of control."

"Aha, now here's the real issue. You're a control freak."
Melanie grinned.

"And you're just trying to cause trouble."

"You've been talking to my family."

"I don't have to talk to your family to recognize a mischief
maker when I see one."

"Here, come help me." She turned and sauntered over to
the prep area, knowing he would follow. No matter how
much he might be fighting it, he was hooked.

"You're used to getting your way," he said, coming to
stand beside her.

"So?" Melanie didn't answer Robert as she washed her
hands at the prep sink.

"You've gotten by on your charm for a long time."

"What's wrong with that?"

"Not everyone understands that charm doesn't equal sin-
cerity. How many hearts have you broken along the way with
that come-hither smile of yours?"

Melanie paused. Had she broken a lot of hearts with her
casual flirtations? She'd never really thought about it
before. Was that what she was trying to do with Robert?
Break his heart?

He leaned in close to her the way she'd leaned toward him
earlier, except he actually touched his lips to her ear. "Here's
a heads-up. Turn on all the charm you want, wild thing. I'm
not sleeping with you."

CHAPTER SIX

MUCH TO ROBERT'S SURPRISE, the chocolate turkey turned out to be a hit. Going over the night's receipts, he discovered that forty-seven people had ordered the special. Melanie had been right and he'd been wrong. Roasted turkey, feta cheese, dark chocolate and cayenne pepper. Who would have imagined that bizarre combo would be so popular?

His sassy sous-chef, that's who. Apparently, he'd underestimated the sophistication of Chez Remy customers.

Melanie one, Robert zero.

No, not zero. He'd definitely scored a win when he'd informed her that he would not sleep with her.

His pronouncement had taken her aback. He'd seen surprise in the widening of her indigo eyes. She wasn't accustomed to being refused.

Melanie one, Robert one.

Whose ball was the court in now?

It's not a game. Stop thinking about Melanie and get down to work.

He liked doing paperwork in the quiet hours late at night, after the rest of the staff had gone home. He found the silence peaceful. He wrote out a purchase order for ten cases of feta cheese and dark chocolate. Chocolate turkey was officially on the menu. He took a sip of his tepid coffee. The radio on his desk was in the middle of a sports recap on satellite talk radio, but tonight Robert was in the mood for music. Something light and fast. He picked up the remote control and skimmed through the channels.

An old song by the Trogs caught his attention because it reminded him of Melanie. "Wild Thing." Smiling, he left the dial on the station.

He was half listening to the song, half concentrating on filling out the form, when he heard a noise in the empty kitchen. He'd thought everyone was gone for the night. Was someone still here? Frowning, he immediately thought of the recent mishaps at the hotel.

The sound came again.

A thumping noise from the dry-storage pantry.

No matter what story he'd concocted for Jeri Kay Loving, Robert didn't believe in poltergeists. Someone was rummaging around in the pantry.

A thief?

Quietly, he eased his chair away from the desk. Muscles tensed, ears cocked, he rose to his feet. Creeping on the balls of his feet, he edged toward his door.

Thump, thump.

He glanced around for a weapon, saw nothing in his office that would suffice, but thought of the rolling pins kept mounted above the pastry chef's workstation. That would do.

The door creaked when he turned the knob and eased it open. He froze in the doorway, listening intently, waiting to see if he'd been overheard by the intruder.

Save for a night-light over the stove, the restaurant was dark The rustling came from the pantry once more.

Gotcha.

He sneaked toward the pastry chef's workstation and lifted the heftiest rolling pin from its place on the pegboard. Wielding it like a baseball bat, Robert rushed to the pantry.

"Stop right there," he hollered, at the same moment Melanie let out a shriek.

They stared at each other.

"Oh," they said in unison. "It's you."

Melanie's hand was splayed across her heart.

Robert lowered the rolling pin.

"What are you doing here?" they said simultaneously, and then both laughed shakily.

"You gave me a start," Melanie said breathlessly.

"I thought you were a thief." Robert shook his head ruefully. "You just missed getting bashed with a rolling pin."

He swept his gaze over her and realized she'd been unloading a dolly stacked with boxes of canned goods. A Swiss Army knife lay open on the floor beside her. She seemed to have been in the process of slicing the tape off the top box.

"What's this?" he asked.

"Late delivery," she said. "I discovered this order sitting outside the service entrance as I was leaving."

"Was it an expected order?"

"Yes. I thought you were already gone. You might want to check out the delivery doorbell. I doubt it's working. I didn't hear it buzz all night. Guess the delivery guy just gave up and left it there."

"I'll check it out."

She glanced over at him and he could swear that just for a moment he caught a glimpse of nervousness in her eyes. What was she afraid of? Being startled by him wielding a rolling pin? Or being alone in the kitchen with him late at night?

But the look quickly vanished.

"I'll help you." He rolled up his sleeves and moved into the narrow ten-by-four-foot pantry with her.

"That's okay. I've got it under control. You go on home." Melanie grabbed a couple of jars of pickles from the box and bent to shelve them, presenting him with a great view of her jean-clad backside.

"A good boss doesn't leave until after his last employee does." He squeezed around the dolly and came to stand beside her.

"I heard it the other way around. A good employee stays until her boss goes home."

"At this rate," he chuckled, "neither one of us will be leaving tonight."

Leaning in, he picked up a couple of pickle jars to shelve, and his shoulder brushed lightly against hers. Sexual tension snapped like static electricity. Purposefully, he ignored the jolt of awareness, even though it twisted him up like a pretzel.

"Thanks for offering to help, but I can finish this up on my own. It won't take me ten minutes for the rest."

"You've got four more boxes to unload."

"It'll go faster if I do it by myself. I've got a system."

"What's the matter, Melanie?" he asked. "Do I make you nervous?"

She rolled her eyes. "No."

"I think I make you nervous."

"You *don't* make me nervous," she reiterated. Picking up her Swiss Army knife, she cut open the second box, then closed the blade and pocketed it.

"Why do you shy away every time our shoulders brush?" he asked.

"I don't like being crowded."

"You didn't seem to mind so much last night when you were crowding me."

"That was different."

"Do you want to know what I think?"

"Not really, but I have a feeling you're going to tell me anyway," she said.

"I think you kissed me simply to prove to yourself that I don't make you nervous."

Melanie snorted. "That's ridiculous. You were the one who kissed *me*."

"You kissed me back."

"What if I did?"

"Then why resist my help?"

"Fine." She threw her hands in the air. "Go ahead, help away."

She stepped toward the door.

"Where are you going?"

"Leaving it to you," she said tartly. "Obviously you're such a control freak you don't trust me to shelve canned goods correctly."

"I trust you."

"It doesn't feel like it."

"Maybe you think I don't trust you because deep down inside you feel as if *you're* not trustworthy."

"What? That's insane." Melanie denied it, but she didn't meet his eyes, and he had a feeling his comment had struck the mark.

"Is it?"

"Totally."

Their hands touched as they both reached for the same restaurant-size can of tomatoes, and instantly, Melanie jumped back. She was edgy as a cat.

Then again, so was he.

"I think an assembly line is in order," Robert suggested. "It'll be quicker. I'll take the cans out of the box and pass them on to you to shelve."

Robert passed her the can, she shelved it and they went on to the next item. He tried not to notice how gracefully she moved or how her ponytail spun jauntily about her shoulders. He tried to block the sexual thoughts swimming dangerously in his brain, tried to make himself stop feeling anything for her, particularly while they were in such close quarters together.

Mayonnaise and ketchup and olives. Soon the boxes were empty and Melanie turned back to look at him again.

And his heart sort of slipped sideways in his chest. An iceberg starting to melt.

She was so beautiful. So completely enticing. Her mouth was soft and her eyes softer, and the two of them were standing together in a small pantry in the middle of a quiet, dark kitchen.

Alone.

If he kissed her, no one would ever know.

You would know and she would know.

Yeah, but beyond that.

"Ever been kissed in a supply pantry before?" she asked, reading his thoughts.

"No," he said. "Have you? No, scratch that. I can figure it out for myself. No need to confess your scullery romances."

"I've done a lot more than kiss in a supply pantry, if you know what I mean."

"I get it." He shoved his hands into his pockets and wondered why he felt so damn jealous. Nothing was happening the way he intended.

She shook her head and grinned as if enjoying an inside joke.

"What?"

"How did you get to be thirty—what? One, two?"

"Thirty-two."

"How did you get to be thirty-two and an executive chef without making out in a supply closet?"

He shrugged. "Reverence for canned goods?"

She laughed and the sound lit him up inside.

"Believe me," he said. "I've done plenty of other things."

"Like what?"

"I had sex in an elevator once."

"Ooh, LeSoeur, I'm impressed. Wouldn't have thought you had it in you. Unless you were alone, that is. You weren't alone, were you?" she teased.

"No, I wasn't alone. What's the deal, Melanie? You seem to be under the impression that I'm some sort of soulless drone or a socially inept recluse."

"No." She shook her head. "Not at all. I just think you're a control freak with a brooding streak."

She was right. He was.

Melanie tilted her head as if she was sizing him up. "What do you have to brood about, Robert? What's got you locked up so tight?"

She took the index finger of her right hand and pressed it against his sternum. It was as if in that one crystal moment she knew all his secrets and they did not scare her.

The look in her eyes cajoled him. *Come on, you can tell me anything and I promise I won't judge you. Just be honest with me.*

But he could not trust that look. Nor his sudden impulse to open his mouth and tell her why he was the way he was. Why he needed control.

Being orphaned at an early age had cursed him with a loneliness he feared he would never shake. He'd done his best to overcome the tragedy of his childhood, but even twenty years later, a sadness could unexpectedly clamp down on him like a cold hand.

Maybe that was one of the reasons he was so attracted to Melanie. She was so warm. Like a cozy fireplace greeting a weary traveler coming in from the cold. He saw in her and her closeknit family something he had never had, but always longed for. A sense of connection. Belonging.

She'd pegged him to a tee.

In a rush, it swept through him. His loneliness, his need, his haunting desire for her.

Without preamble, he claimed her mouth with his, surprising them both.

"Oh," Melanie whispered, then mumbled, "You taste good."

"Hush, woman," he growled, and their lips vibrated with the sound. He kissed her deeply, savoring the heat of her mouth and pulling her up tight against his chest.

His rational mind was telling him he shouldn't be doing this, that he was going to regret it as soon as it was over, but his soul was whispering, *Let go, take a chance*.

He closed his eyes. She tasted so sweet and she felt so good in his arms that it blanked out all coherent thought.

Tongues and mouths and teeth and heat.

He was submerged.

Gone under. Drowning. Happily drowning.

Fight it.

But he couldn't. He didn't want to fight it. It had been too long and it felt incredible, and he was just a man, lonely and looking for a light to lead him out of the blackness.

Abruptly, she pulled back.

He opened his eyes, hardly able to focus, his breathing reedy, his mouth tingling.

She stood looking at him, her hair tousled, her chest rising and falling from her fast, gasping breath.

"What was that?" she whispered.

"What was what?"

"Didn't you hear it?"

"Hear what?" He hadn't heard anything beyond the pounding of blood rushing through his ears.

"Someone's in the kitchen," she said.

He was facing the shelving, his back to the pantry door. Robert cocked his head, listening.

Nothing.

"I don't hear anything."

"Shh." She pressed her index finger against her lips. Lips that seconds ago he'd been kissing with the abandon of a monk who'd forsaken his religious vows.

They waited.

He heard it.

The sound of footfalls.

Quick, furtive, close.

Melanie mouthed a question. "Do you think it's—"

Robert spun around just as the pantry door slammed closed.

And then came the solid clicking of the lock being turned.

SIMULTANEOUSLY, they bolted for the door, reaching for the knob at the same time. Robert got there first and Melanie's hand clamped over his.

Together, they turned it, but the knob would not budge.

They were locked in.

It was long after midnight. No one was around to hear their cries for help.

They were trapped, with no way out.

Impossible. They couldn't be trapped.

Panic started to rise in Melanie. Suddenly, she was a kid again, on that trip to the Grand Canyon, crowded into the back of the camper with her sisters and with only one tiny window too high to peer out. The memory hit her hard, and she felt as if she were smothering.

Perspiration popped out on her forehead and she clawed at the collar of her shirt, trying to tear it open, to get free.

"Hey, hey." Robert grabbed her hand. "What is it? What's wrong?"

"Claustrophobic," she gasped. "Air, I need air."

"Look." He cupped her chin, forced her to look up at the ceiling. "It's vented in here. We won't run out of air."

"Hot." She fanned herself. "So hot."

"Yes, you are."

She sent him a black look. "Don't make fun. I mean it. I feel like I'm burning up inside."

"Calm down." He ripped a section of cardboard off one of the boxes and fanned her with it. "Take a deep breath. That's it. There's no reason to panic. You're safe."

"But we're locked in a small space."

"Not that small. We could lie down in here. Make a bed

of those flour sacks. It's okay. We have food and water, and someone will be along in the morning to let us out. It's okay."

It didn't feel okay, but Robert's eyes were full of sympathy. He was right. She needed to get a grip on this thing before it pulled her down completely.

But she didn't know how. She was trying to take deep breaths, but it wasn't working. Her mind kept fixating on the walls, how narrow they were. They seemed to be closing in on her.

Stop freaking out.

"Help!" she cried, and pounded on the door with both fists. "Help, help, we're locked in. Get us out of here!"

"Hey, hey." Robert grabbed her shoulders and spun her around. "It's okay."

It wasn't okay. He didn't understand. She felt like she was on the *Titanic* and dark, icy waters were rolling in over her head.

"I have to get out, I have to get out," she babbled, unable to stop.

Still gripping her by the shoulders, Robert smashed his mouth against hers, taking control. She knew he was kissing her in an attempt to shock her out of her panic attack, and the hell of it was, his ploy worked. His brashness comforted her.

Involuntarily, her body softened in his arms and she opened her mouth, letting him in.

Lip therapy as a cure for claustrophobia.

Who knew?

Of course, a kiss had started this whole mess. If he hadn't been kissing her in the first place, they wouldn't be locked in here.

Their lips fit so perfectly together, snug as the right lid on a pot, that Melanie stopped trembling. She kept her eyes open because she was afraid closing them would make the claustrophobia worse.

His eyes were open, too, whereas before he'd closed them. He was watching her intently, gauging her reaction, trying to see if she was calming down. That alone was both strangely reassuring and wildly arousing.

A scorching heat flashed through her, hot and fast, incinerating everything in its path—her tongue, her throat, her chest and beyond. She burned from the glorious pressure of his lips.

Ached for him

She was almost thirty years old and she'd been married and divorced. She'd had her fair share of admirers.

But this kiss!

It was even more powerful than the one they'd shared the night before.

He groaned low in his throat. His body strained and pushed against hers.

Melanie met him measure for measure, reaching up to cup his face in her palms, marveling at the feel of his warm skin.

He breathed her name, and she moaned quietly.

Melanie's need was out of control. Excitement warred with guilt and passion. She wanted to laugh. She wanted to cry. She wanted to run. That's what she'd always done when she got in over her head.

Except this time there was nowhere to go. This time she had to face her fears and deal with them.

Okay. She could do this. Resolutely, she pulled her lips away from his and drew in a shuddering breath.

Robert ran his hands down her arms and stepped back, almost bumping into the green metal dolly. "Feeling better?"

"Much. Thank you." Strangely, she did feel better. His kiss had knocked her right out of the panic zone.

Robert moved the dolly over into the corner and re-arranged the sacks of flour that had been stacked under the bottom shelf to make a pallet for them on the floor.

"Come sit down," he said, and held out a hand to her.

She eased down beside him and took a shaky breath. They sat with their backs propped against the wall, legs stretched out over the fifty-pound sacks.

"It's going to be okay."

"I wish I had my cell phone. Normally I carry it strapped to my waistband, but since I was leaving for the night I stuck it in my purse. Then I found the boxes at the service entrance."

"Hmm." Robert looked thoughtful.

"What?"

"I'm wondering if the boxes being left outside for you to find, and us being locked in, wasn't a coincidence," he said.

"You're thinking it might have something to do with the problems we've had lately with some of our other orders?" There had been mix-ups with coffee deliveries that Robert had blamed on their supplier, but now Melanie wondered if someone else had intentionally interfered with the orders. And obviously the person who'd locked them in here didn't want to be identified.

Robert draped an arm over her shoulder. "Now you're starting to sound paranoid," he teased her, freeing her hair from its ponytail and weaving his fingers through the silky strands to shake it loose about her shoulders. He looked at her, his irises darkened with pleasure.

Melanie stared back, hardly able to breathe, then had to look away. She curled her hands into fists, but couldn't resist glancing furtively at Robert. He was still staring at her.

Incredulous.

There was no mistaking the spark of sexual attraction on his face. Desire shadowed his eyes, giving him a lean and dangerous look.

This had nothing to do with her attack of claustrophobia. Robert seemed quite turned on by the fact that they were locked up tight in the supply closet.

Melanie could smell the delicious kitchen scent on his skin and wondered how many women before her had been this close to him.

"Robert…"

What was she going to say? She reached out, not knowing what she intended to do, caught up in the crazy push-pull battle inside her.

What did she want from him? Did she want them to be colleagues with a good relationship, working together to make Chez Remy an even better restaurant than it already was? Or did she want to get rid of him so she could run the place by herself?

Or did she want to be his lover?

The thought of the last option both scared and excited her.

Who was this man?

She didn't know much about him. All she knew was that when she was with him, she felt a sense of something larger, something beyond them both. She felt a connection that had been missing in her life, and yet she was afraid to trust the feeling. She thought she'd found it once before with David, and she'd been so wrong.

Yeah, but that was different.

With her ex-husband it had been all about the red-hot sex. They'd burned brightly, but reality had quickly snuffed out the passion. With Robert, she saw that there could be so much more. He possessed so many layers…so many secrets. She yearned to explore them all, bit by bit, peeling back each one until she found his core and understood who he really was.

It was a gripping idea. One she seemed powerless to fight. She had an overwhelming urge to know him inside and out but why?

Helplessly, she reached out to touch his scar.

Robert raised an arm, blocking her hand. He was breathing hard and didn't speak. He didn't have to. She could read the message in his eyes loud and clear.

I want to take you to bed.

The thrill that raced through her body was so powerful she almost orgasmed right there on the spot.

There it was. They'd been avoiding this for months, trying to ignore this burning attraction.

His eyes were inscrutable, giving nothing away, but he was still combing his fingers through her hair, lulling her.

She had to find a way to distract him. If he kept touching her like that she was going to get naked with him real quick, and as appealing as that seemed, she wasn't ready. Not this way. Not here in the supply pantry.

Not yet.

Not until she resolved for herself what it was she really wanted from him.

She opened her mouth to tell Robert this, but then he kissed her again and all her resistance vanished.

CHAPTER SEVEN

LIKE AN ADDICT IN NEED OF a fix, Robert was compelled to take another taste of her, even though the smart side of his brain was hollering at him to stop.

How could he stop when she was so eager and responding so sweetly? When his body ached to be melded with hers?

She touched him eagerly, easily, one hand cupping the back of his head, the other sliding around his waist.

Melanie was kissing him back. Kissing him as if it were the end of the world and they the only two survivors. It would be so easy to make love to her right here, right now.

Too damn easy.

Her soft fingertips were like instruments of delicious torture, tracking up the skin of his bare forearms, coaxing open the buttons of his shirt, reaching inside to playfully tug at his chest hairs.

He groaned when she pulled her lips from his and began nibbling her way down the length of his throat, planting firebrand kisses with her hot mouth.

"Robert," she murmured. "Robert."

Her sigh of need was an arrow straight through him, and the whisper of his name on her lips, said with such ecstasy, let him know that she was his for the taking.

In the past, he hadn't had much luck with long-term relationships. The problems lay as much with him as with the women he picked. A month or two into it and he would grow bored and restless, knowing there should be so much more, but too afraid of losing control to let himself go for it.

But over the course of the last four months, working side by side with Melanie, he'd found himself spellbound. He'd never felt anything like it. No woman had ever challenged him the way she did. None had jettisoned his arousal to such heights, leaving him weak-kneed and desperate for more. Quite simply, he had never wanted a woman the way he wanted Melanie.

Hold on to your control, LeSoeur.

But holding on to his control was difficult to do when he was locked in a closet with the sexiest woman he'd ever come across. Especially when he wanted so badly to let go. He'd been holding on tightly for so many years. Keeping his emotions bottled up inside, too afraid of the potential pain to allow himself to feel too deeply. Using his journal as a release valve. But it was no longer working.

She kissed his bare chest and brushed her fingertips past the flat of his belly to the zipper of his pants. He closed his eyes, trying to hold on to his last shred of control.

He groaned.

"Do you like that?"

"I like it too damn much. You're going to have to stop doing that."

She just giggled and ran her tongue around his navel.

Robert hissed in a breath and closed his eyes.

Fight it off.

But he was just a man, and what she was doing felt so

good. This wasn't just any woman. It was Melanie, the woman he'd been harboring secret fantasies about for months.

"Oh my," she said. "Look what just popped up." She started inching his zipper down with her index finger and thumb.

He clamped his teeth together and forced himself to grab her wrist. If he didn't halt her now, he could not be held accountable for what happened next.

"You're going to have to stop doing that," Robert rasped, barely able to breathe. He felt as if he was going to explode.

"Why's that?" she murmured, her voice thick and husky with emotion.

"No condom," he said simply, although his reasons for asking her to stop were myriad. Lack of protection was the one argument she could not refute.

"Oh." She took in a shaky breath. "I hadn't thought that far in advance."

"Obviously not." Truth be told, neither had he. The way he was feeling, if he'd known an intruder was going to lock them in the supply pantry together, he would have crammed his pockets full of condoms.

"You know," she said, wriggling her eyebrows and looking completely adorable, "there are other things we can do. If you get my drift."

"I know." He swallowed hard.

"But you don't want to do those things, either?"

"I want to. Very much."

"Me, too, Robert. I'm hot for you." She slowly unbuttoned her shirt, giving him a scrumptious view of her pink lace bra and lovely cleavage.

He forced himself to avert his eyes. "I'm hot for you, too, babe, but I'm not sure this is what either of us really wants."

"Trust me on this. I want you. Bad."

"It's just the proximity."

"It's not. I've been having X-rated dreams about you for weeks."

"So you *were* dreaming about me." He smiled.

"Every friggin' night. Now come on, please, put me out of my misery."

"Sorry. You're too vulnerable. Ten minutes ago claustrophobia had you flipping out." He wished she'd stop trying to convince him. Couldn't she tell he was hanging by a thread?

"I'm all better now."

"I don't want you regretting this in the morning."

"Life's too short for regrets. That's my motto." She was still kissing him, running her tongue along the inside of his jaw.

"Melanie," he said sharply. "You're killing me here. You might not regret it tomorrow, but what if I do?"

"Oh," she said, and blinked at him.

"I like you too much. I don't want to ruin that."

"So once you sleep with me, you can't like me anymore?"

"No, no. That's not what I'm saying. Look, if it happens between us, I want it to be right. I don't want it be something we do just because we're locked up together with nothing else to do."

"I see."

"I've hurt your feelings."

"No. I get it. You don't do spontaneous."

He started to argue, but maybe she was right. Maybe the reason his conscience wouldn't let him follow through with this was because it felt too fast, too spur-of-the-moment. Mentally, he needed more time. Convincing his body of that was a whole other issue, however. But it was up to him to put on the brakes. He was the rational one here.

"Let's just get some sleep." He took her by the shoulders and moved her away from him so he could button up his shirt.

"You're probably right," she said, but the expression in her eyes told Robert that she thought he was totally wrong. "No worries. I'm officially not turned on anymore."

He wished he could say the same, but then he caught the furtive look in her eyes and knew she was lying.

"Will you be all right, claustrophobia-wise, if I turn off the overhead light?"

"I think so," she said. "I hope so."

Me, too, he thought. *I'd hate to have to keep kissing you all night to stop you from panicking.*

He knew he couldn't do that. His self-control had been tested to its outer limits and if they did any more kissing, he would slip right over the edge.

He got up, walked to the wall and switched off the light, plunging them into blackness. He heard Melanie's sharp intake of breath and realized she was struggling not to panic again.

"You okay?" he asked, reaching out to run his fingers along the wall shelving to guide him as he headed back toward her.

"I'm okay," she echoed. "I'm trying to pretend I'm at home in my own bed. Except if I were at home, you wouldn't be there, of course."

"Sounds like a solid plan. Go with that." His foot bumped into a flour sack.

"Here," she said. "Take my hand and I'll help you down."

That was exactly what he was afraid of. That she would pull him down to a place where he had no business being. In the inky blackness, she reached toward him and touched his hip.

He took her hand and slowly sank down. The flour sacks were short and he ended up having to bend his knees to keep his legs from hanging over the edge.

The quarters were cramped. He and Melanie had to touch, it was an inescapable reality. He lay on his back beside her, feeling the cottony material of her blouse against his shoulder, hearing the sound of her uneven breathing, smelling the sweet womanly scent of her.

He was more aware of her than he was of himself. He wanted to roll over and nuzzle her neck so badly he had to clench his hands into fists to keep from doing so, holding tight to his last shred of control. Turning off the light hadn't been such a hot idea, after all.

It's for her benefit, not yours. Be a man, suck it up.

And he did, because that's what he was good at—sucking up his pain, holding out in the face of powerful temptation. It had gotten him this far in life, why mess with a sure thing?

"I'm trying hard not to think about it," Melanie murmured. "But I keep imagining that the walls are closing in on us, getting smaller and smaller. Like in a haunted house."

"Picture something else. Visualize a new recipe. What's your next great creation?"

"I was thinking cherry salmon."

"Hmm…sounds interesting. Tell me about it."

"Rainier cherries and wild Pacific Coast salmon poached in a nice Riesling, then garnished with slivered chestnuts and crumbled Roquefort cheese." Her breathing slowed as she spoke. "I'm thinking it's past time for a Northwestern influence here in New Orleans. We could call it salmon Le-Soeur."

He didn't know why he found the idea of Melanie naming her recipe in honor of him so touching, but he did. "Have you tried it out?"

"Not yet. Maybe you could come over to my apartment sometime and we could make it together."

"Are you inviting me on a date?"

"Do you want me to invite you on a date?"

Did he?

The sound of her breathing picked up. Went raspy and irregular. He figured she was giving in to her claustrophobia again.

"Stop visualizing the walls closing in on you," he commanded.

"How did you know that's what I was doing?" Her voice sounded odd. Was it fear? Or something else?

"I'm getting pretty accomplished at reading you, Melanie Marchand."

"Now that's a scary thought." She sounded like her old self.

"Would you like me to turn the light back on?"

"No, no, that's okay. I can handle it." Her breathing chugged faster.

"Melanie, are you all right?"

"Could I…um…just…,"

"Just what?"

"Would you mind if I rested my head on your chest? I hate being such a baby, but I think I would feel safer."

"Sure," he said, even though he wanted to tell her no for

the sake of his sanity. He dropped his arm around her shoulder and pulled her against him. She shifted her head, her silky hair trailing over his skin.

She might feel safer, but *he* didn't. Robert had to bite down on his bottom lip to hold back a groan of pleasure as her body heat warmed him. The last thing he wanted was to get things stirred up between them again.

"May I ask you a personal question?" she ventured several minutes later.

"You can ask."

"But you might not answer."

"That's right."

"Fair enough."

"What's the question?"

"Why did you move to New Orleans?"

"Your mother offered me my dream job."

"There's more to it than that," she said, tracing a circle over his heart with the tip of her finger.

Stop doing that, he wanted to shout. *Please stop doing that. You're pushing me to the edge of reason, woman.* But he said nothing, not wanting her to know exactly how much power she had over him. Revealing your weaknesses was never a good idea.

"I needed a fresh start," he said.

"Fresh start? From what?"

"You sure ask a lot of questions."

"I know it's none of my business, but I've worked with you for four months and I hardly know anything personal about you—well, except for how you lost your virginity—and I'm curious what makes you tick. Was there something you were running away from? Say, a scandal, perhaps?"

He laughed. "A scandal? Me? Sorry to disappoint you, but no scandal. I guess I'd finally just had enough rain in my life."

"That's it?"

"That's it," he lied.

The thing of it was, Robert didn't like talking about his past. It was over and done with. No use crying over spilled milk and all that.

"Oh. I forgot to tell you," Melanie said, before he could decide what and how much to divulge to her about his past. "I need to switch my day off from tomorrow to Thursday."

"No problem. I'll cover for you."

"You're sure it's okay? Because I have to do this thing for Charlotte."

"We'll be fine. Go do what you need to do."

"I don't want to do what I need to do," she said glumly.

"What is it that you have to do?"

"I told Charlotte I'd be her stand-in at a silly bachelor-ette auction."

"A bachelorette auction?"

"It's for a charity that my grandmother Celeste runs, so it's pretty difficult to get out of it." Melanie groaned. "I really hate these uptight, stuffed shirt, high society shindigs. My sisters were all debutantes, but not me. Luckily, by the time I came along, my grand-mère had gotten it out of her system and pretty well let me be."

"Men will be bidding on a date with you?" Robert's voice rose slightly. He hated the idea of Melanie being up for grabs to the highest bidder, worthy charity or not.

"Yes."

"I don't like the sound of that."

"Why, Robert, are you jealous?"

He heard the levity in her voice. Was she laughing at him? "Jealous? No, why would I be jealous?" He gritted his teeth.

"Because I'll be spending the evening with another man."

"Maybe we can't spare you in the kitchen, after all," Robert said. "Come to think of it, we're going to be very busy on Thursday night."

"Nice try, but I really do have to go to this thing. I have to prove to my family that they can depend on me to do what I say I'll do."

"Why's that?"

"I'm the baby and I have something of a reputation for being irresponsible. I call it youthful indiscretion. My family calls it a pattern."

"You're very lucky to have a family who cares so much about you."

"I know, but sometimes being part of a big family can get a little…well, claustrophobic, which is why I left New Orleans the day I turned eighteen. How about you? What did your family think about you moving to New Orleans?"

"I don't have a family," he said bluntly. "Not anymore. Only child. Both my parents are dead."

"Oh, Robert."

The sympathy in her voice was real and he was touched by it. He felt the growing bond between them strengthen. "It was a long time ago."

"I'm so sorry. I know how badly it hurts to lose a parent, but to lose them both when you're so young…"

"I've dealt with it," he said gruffly.

"That explains a lot."

"How so?"

"Why you can be so distant and brooding at times. Why

you bury yourself in your work. It's an escape for you, isn't it?"

"Work is work—I don't use it as an escape." But he knew that wasn't true.

"So when do you play?"

"I'm not much for idle pastimes."

"What you're saying is you don't know how to have fun. Your childhood got ruined and you never learned how to play, did you?"

"No, I didn't have a fun and sunny childhood." He didn't like being psychoanalyzed.

"I could teach you," she said. "How to have fun, I mean."

"Maybe I don't want to learn."

"You only say that because you've never really had any fun. I can tell."

"Shh, go to sleep," he said. She was not only right but very perceptive.

"You're weird, you know that? I could be locked in here with a dozen different guys and every single one of them would crumble. What makes you so in control, Robert? Or is it that you just don't have any feelings? Are you mannequin man?"

She was trying to goad him into making love to her, but he would not fall for it. He bit down hard on the inside of his cheek to keep from grabbing her and giving her exactly what she wanted.

Silence loomed, a tangible thing.

"You still awake?" she whispered a few minutes later.

He didn't answer, pretending to be asleep, and eventually she stilled. With a mixture of regret and relief, he lay listening to the soft sounds of her breathing.

Melanie's body was firmly muscled, yet at the same time softly curved. She was uninhibited about her sexuality, and that fact alone unnerved him. He was outclassed and out of his league, and he knew it. His last few relationships had been with calm, studious women who could either take sex or leave it. And that was what Robert told himself he wanted.

The gleam in Melanie's eyes whenever he kissed her told him she cared about sex and cared deeply. How could he ever hope to measure up to her expectations? Or satisfy her sexually? She thrived on thrills and excitement, and he was as dull as they came.

But he wanted her so much his mind was muddled and his heart actually hurt.

Which was exactly the quandary.

He wanted her. He couldn't have her. She was all wrong for him and he was all wrong for her. He didn't do runaway lust and she didn't do commitment.

He was just experiencing a physical reaction. Chemistry. It meant nothing.

"Absolutely nothing."

But even as he whispered the words in the darkness, Robert knew they simply weren't true.

MELANIE COULDN'T SLEEP.

Not with her head resting on Robert's hard-muscled chest. Not when she could hear the steady beat of his heart vibrating up through his rib cage and into her ear. Not when her feelings were so muddled.

It seemed her world as she knew it was slowly shifting, and she didn't know whether to embrace what she was feeling or run away from it. On the one hand she loved the novelty of a new experience. On the other, these feelings for Robert scared Melanie more than she cared to admit.

You're just horny, she tried to tell herself. *Robert is sexy as hell and it's been a very long time since you've been with a man. That's all it is.*

How she wanted that to be true. But it wasn't. Like it or not, something important had changed between them. She was both alarmed and exhilarated by the prospect.

Hours passed. Dawn couldn't be far away. Melanie was lying there, wondering how Robert could sleep so soundly on the very lumpy flour sacks, in the stuffy room, when she heard a noise in the kitchen.

The hairs on her arms lifted and she held her breath, straining to listen. Was it the person who'd locked them in here together? Her heart thumped and she sat up.

"Robert," she whispered urgently, and poked him in the ribs. The darkness was so complete she couldn't see him.

He grunted.

"Wake up."

"Huh?"

"There's someone in the kitchen."

"Melanie? What's going on?" He sounded sleep-addled, confused.

"We got locked in the pantry together. Remember?"

"Oh. Right."

"And there's someone in the kitchen," she repeated. She felt him push up on his elbows beside her.

"Hey!" he shouted. "We're locked in."

"Shh, what if it's the guy?"

"What guy?"

"I don't know. The guy who's going around causing trouble at the hotel."

"How do you know—never mind." He took her hand and they struggled to their feet in the darkness, stumbling over the flour sacks.

"Ow! Son of a—" Robert swore darkly.

"What is it?"

"My shin hit the dolly."

Just then the pantry door was wrenched open, light from the kitchen filling the tiny room. Melanie blinked against the sudden illumination, trying to make out who was standing in the doorway.

It was Luc Carter, the hotel concierge.

Luc was blond and blue-eyed like Robert, but slightly shorter and, in Melanie's estimation at least, not nearly as sexy. Melanie preferred Robert's more rugged looks to Luc's almost too perfect features. Luc was a likable, easygoing guy, but Melanie found herself wondering what he was doing in the kitchen so early in the morning.

"What's going on?" Luc asked.

"We got locked in." Robert stifled a yawn.

"You've been here all night?" Luc glanced from Robert to Melanie, and a bemused smile crossed his face. She could see from the expression in his eyes that he was putting two and two together and coming up with a very steamy scenario.

"Yeah." Robert ran a hand through his hair.

"Wild." Luc's grin widened.

"What time is it?" Robert asked.

"Five-thirty. How'd you get locked in?" Luc frowned and studied the locking mechanism on the door.

Robert clued him in about the delivery being left unattended on the loading dock and someone shutting them up inside the pantry together.

"You should probably let security know, but if nothing's been touched in the kitchen, it sounds like a harmless prank." Luc shrugged.

"Not so harmless when you consider Melanie's claustrophobic." Robert's words were like an accusation.

"You are?" Luc looked genuinely surprised. "I didn't know that."

"Why don't we all just keep this to ourselves?" Melanie said. "Maybe it *was* one of the kitchen staff pulling a prank. No point in worrying Charlotte for nothing."

"Agreed," Robert said.

Luc nodded.

"You're here awfully early," Melanie said to Luc. "Working overtime?"

"Charlotte asked me to come in early all week. Just your luck I came through the kitchen on my way to the bar to get a can of Bloody Mary mix for an early-rising guest who indulged too much last night and wanted a little hair of the dog. Otherwise you guys would have been stuck in here until the kitchen staff showed up."

"Just our luck," Robert echoed, and Melanie couldn't help wondering if he suspected that Luc was the one who'd locked them in.

She gave herself a shake. Spending a night in the pantry seemed to have left her delusional as well as exhausted.

CHAPTER EIGHT

IT WAS JUST AFTER 6:00 a.m. when Melanie got home, hoping to grab a nap before she had to be back at the restaurant by noon. She kicked off her shoes and had just opened a can of cat food for the mewling kitten when her doorbell rang.

Who could that be at this hour of the morning?

She padded to the door, peered through the peephole and saw Charlotte standing on her landing, holding a garment bag. Rats, she'd forgotten about the dress for the charity auction.

Sighing, she opened the door.

Charlotte stared at her, eyes widening. "Mel? Mellie?" she asked, calling her by her childhood nickname. "Are you okay? You look…well, as if you've been up all night."

Her gaze lingered on Melanie's top. Melanie glanced down and saw that the buttons were in the wrong holes. She'd buttoned up in the dark last night and hadn't noticed. Trust her eagle-eyed sister not to miss a thing.

"I didn't know you were coming by so early." Melanie ran a hand through her hair. She debated whether to straighten the buttons, but decided at this point it would call more attention to her disheveled appearance than if she ignored them.

"You look like you've been up all night partying." Charlotte pressed her lips into a thin line.

Melanie almost told her about getting locked in the pantry with Robert, but decided against it—whether because of the twitch at the corner of Charlotte's mouth, or the fact that she hadn't yet sorted out her feelings about what happened between herself and Robert.

"I didn't sleep well," she mumbled. That was true enough. No lie there. Who could sleep with raging hormones and no outlet for them, while trapped in a supply closet for hours with a very sexy man?

"Are you going to invite me in?" Charlotte lifted an eyebrow.

Melanie's place was a mess. She hadn't cleaned in days, but she couldn't very well leave her sister standing on the landing. Melanie stood aside. "Come on in."

Charlotte stepped over the threshold. "Oh look, you've got a kitten." She draped the garment bag over the back of a kitchen chair and reached down to pick up the furry animal. She glanced up at Melanie, a happy smile on her face.

"She's not my kitten. She showed up on the doorstep a couple of days ago and I haven't had a chance to ask around the apartment complex to see if she belongs to anyone."

"Oh." Charlotte set the kitten on the floor and went to the sink to wash up. Melanie could have sworn her sister sounded disappointed, but she couldn't fathom why.

Charlotte eyed the dishes stacked in the sink. She didn't say anything, but the look on her face was enough to make Melanie feel guilty for being such a slob.

"Do you have any coffee?" Charlotte asked. "I'll make a pot of coffee. You look like you could use it."

Melanie groaned inwardly. So much for a nap. "In the pantry," she said.

"Why don't you try on the dress? See if it fits? There's still time to get it altered."

She didn't want to try on the dress, but she also didn't want to upset Charlotte. While her sister rummaged in the pantry for coffee, Melanie took the dress from the garment bag. This time, she did groan out loud. "What's this?"

"What?" Charlotte asked.

Melanie held up the silver, floor-length, strapless taffeta gown.

"You didn't tell me it's a formal event!"

"It's a masquerade ball."

"You've gotta be kidding me."

"You're not thinking of bailing out now?"

"No," Melanie forced herself to reply. "I'm all in."

Charlotte set the coffee on the countertop. "I want you to know I really appreciate you standing in for me. I was pulling out my hair with so many things on my plate and not knowing how I was going to fit this in."

The idea of her perfectly coiffed sister pulling out her hair was ludicrous, but Melanie understood the analogy. Just looking at the taffeta gown was enough to make her want to pull her own hair out. She took a deep breath. *You can do this. It's for charity and earns you brownie points with both Grand-mère and Charlotte.*

"It's no big deal." She shrugged but could not deny the warmth Charlotte's words sparked in her heart.

"Where's the coffeemaker?" Charlotte glanced around the kitchen.

"On the counter underneath the bar."

"I still don't see it."

"Next to the answering machine."

"You keep your answering machine in your kitchen?"

"It's handier here than in the bedroom. I don't have a phone jack in the living room."

"I'm sorry, but I still don't see it."

"It's got tea towels stacked on top of it."

"Ah." Charlotte whipped the towels off the coffeemaker and laid them across the answering machine. "There you are."

She busied herself with measuring out the coffee, and Melanie couldn't help wondering how her sister could look so polished at this time of the morning. She was amazing.

"I suppose I should warn you about something regarding the auction," Charlotte said, without meeting Melanie's eye.

"Don't tell me. There's a matching tiara that comes with the dress."

"No tiara, I promise."

"Then how bad can it be? Besides wearing this dress, I mean." Melanie poked the gown with a finger.

"Wilmer Haddock's going to be there."

"No."

"Sorry."

Melanie covered her head with her arms. "Just kill me now, please."

"Come on, Wilmer's not *that* bad."

"Said by a woman who's never been the object of his affection."

Wilmer Haddock owned a curio shop down the street, and his family had lived in the French Quarter as long as the Marchands. Melanie and Wilmer were the same age and he'd had a crush on her since they were in grade school. When they were fifteen, he'd stuck his hand down her dress at a church picnic, and when she'd slapped his face for it, he actually thought that meant she liked him and was just playing hard to get. He'd never married, and to this day, whenever he saw her, he told her he was waiting for her to come to her senses and realize they were meant to be together.

"Seriously? You're not just teasing me? Wilmer is actually going to be there?"

"You know he belongs to the Historical Restoration So-ciety."

"He only joined to kiss up to Grand-mère Celeste, thinking he could get to me through her. Lucky for me Grand-mère sees right through the unctuous dweeb. He'll bid on me until he outbids everyone else, and I'll be stuck spending the entire night dodging his happy hands."

"You never know. Maybe someone else will bid on you."

"Yeah, right."

"You're not thinking of backing out on me, are you? Because if you are, let me know now. Don't wait until Thursday night when it's too late."

"I'm not backing out on you, Char. Although you could have shared that little tidbit about Wilmer when you asked me to stand in for you."

"I didn't know it then. I just found out yesterday when I was passing by Haddock's Curios and Wilmer came out to tell me how excited he was that you were back home for good."

Melanie pressed her lips tight to keep from groaning again. Well, if nothing else, this would be a true test of her commitment. Sticking out this bachelorette auction should prove to Charlotte that she could depend on her.

Charlotte stood on tiptoes to grab the cups on a shelf that was the perfect height for Melanie's reach, but too high for her much shorter older sister. She lost her balance, wobbled and in the process ended up losing control over the cups. One fell to the counter, landing on the towel covering the answering machine.

"Whew," Charlotte said. "What luck."

"See, if it wasn't for my messy clutter, that cup would be broken now."

"I never said anything about the clutter."

"You didn't have to. You screw up your mouth when you disapprove of something."

"I do?"

"Yup."

The answering machine beeped and they both startled as it began to play her messages.

"Ms. Marchand, this is Tad Lasiter with Chefs-to-Go. I've found the perfect job opportunity for you in Seattle. I'm waiting for your call back." He left a number.

"Chefs to go?" Charlotte raised an eyebrow.

"Headhunter."

"Toots, it's Coby." Her friend's voice spun from the answering machine out into the room. "Have I got the goods for you, and let me just say, it's primo stuff. Call me!"

The machine beeped again as the message ended.

Charlotte looked at Melanie. "Primo stuff?

"A friend scored me some hard-to-find chocolate." Melanie didn't like fibbing, but she certainly wasn't going to tell Charlotte that she'd had Robert investigated. It all seemed so silly now, and pointless. Especially in light of what she and Robert had shared the night before. But from the sound of his voice, Coby had obviously uncovered something juicy.

"You're blushing," Charlotte said.

Melanie raised a hand to her cheek. "I'm not."

"Are you embarrassed?" her sister teased. "Is this friend more than just a friend?"

Coby? It was all she could do not to burst out laughing. Had Charlotte not picked up from the flamboyant quality in Coby's voice that he would never be interested in anything except friendship with a woman?

"Uh, no."

"Hmm, who is he?"

"Coby Harrington. Lives in Seattle."

Charlotte's face fell. "You're not thinking of moving to Seattle for this guy? Is that what the Chefs-to-Go thing was about, too?"

"Charlotte, believe me when I tell you the last thing on my mind is a romance with Coby Harrington."

"Okay, if you say so."

Charlotte poured the coffee and they spent the next few minutes purposely ignoring the tension Coby's message had caused, and chatting about preparations for the Charboneaux-Long wedding. Charlotte was doing everything in her power to ensure that nothing went wrong with this event. Melanie again toyed with the idea of telling her sister about her and Robert getting locked in the pantry at Chez Remy the night before, but decided against it. Charlotte had enough to worry about.

"You never did try on the dress," her sister said.

"It'll fit."

"You're sure you don't want to try it on? I'm a lot shorter than you."

"I can let the hem out on my own," Melanie stated. "And we both wear a size six. It should be fine."

"All right." Charlotte got to her feet. "Thanks again."

"You're welcome." She walked her sister to the door.

The minute Charlotte was gone, Melanie charged to the phone, anxious to call Coby back and find out exactly what he'd unearthed about Robert. She forgot about the time difference, and it took several rings before Coby answered in a grumpy voice.

"This better be important," he groused.

"Coby, it's Melanie. I just got your message."

"Toots, it's almost five o'clock in the morning here. If it wasn't you, I'd hang up and tell you to call back at a human hour."

"I'm really sorry. I didn't stop to factor in the time difference. Forgive me?"

"You're forgiven, but only because this gossip is too juicy for me to pout too long."

"What did you find out about Robert LeSoeur?" she asked. For some crazy reason her pulse sped up, and she could almost feel the hot blood racing through her veins. She tightened her grip on the receiver.

"It's scandal, scandal, scandal."

Now that she'd put all this in motion, she wasn't sure she wanted to hear the scuttlebutt on Robert, but on the other hand she couldn't stand not knowing. "Stop teasing and just tell me."

"Aw, you're no fun."

"Spill it," she growled.

"Okay, here's the deal. Your friend LeSoeur comes from very old money."

"What do you mean?"

"High society, just like your mother's family. Maybe even more so."

"He's rich?"

"Loaded."

"What else?" She couldn't say why she was so impatient, but she wanted to rip the words out of Coby's throat.

"Robert got into some legal trouble when he was eighteen. His aunt, Pamela Longren—"

"Congresswoman Pamela Longren?" Melanie interrupted him.

"That'd be the one. Anyway, at the time Robert got into trouble, she was the local D.A. and she got him off scott-free. She had his record expunged, the whole works."

Melanie inhaled sharply. She wasn't sure she wanted to ask the next question, but she'd taken things this far, so might as well see it through.

"What kind of trouble? What were the charges leveled against him?"

"Guess."

She had to bite her tongue to keep from yelling at Coby. He enjoyed the drama and she *had* woken him up at an indecent hour. "I don't know. He spray-painted obscene graffiti art on a public building?"

"You wish it was that mild."

"He stole a car and went joy-riding."

"Worse."

Melanie closed her eyes and tried to imagine Robert as a teenager. What could he have done that was so bad? He was so controlled. But he did have a brooding side. Her stomach torqued as she imagined the worst. "He killed someone."

"Gosh, no, toots. Take it down a notch. The man's not a gangster."

"What else is there?"

"Come on, you've been in the restaurant business long enough to know the answer."

"Drugs?"

"Ding, ding, ding, give the girl a Kewpie doll."

"What kind of drugs?"

"Guess again."

"Marijuana?"

"Ganja is child's play. Up here the cops don't even spank your hand for that."

Melanie moistened her lips. Her chest was so tight she had trouble drawing in air. She didn't want to believe any of this about Robert. Maybe Coby had made a mistake. Maybe there was another Robert LeSoeur.

"Cocaine?" She exhaled. Her ex-husband had snorted cocaine, and just thinking of Robert messing around with the stuff made her feel sick to her stomach.

"Bingo," Coby said. "Want to know what else?"

"I want everything you've got," she said. "All of it."

CHARLOTTE SAT IN THE CAR outside Melanie's apartment, keys clutched in her hand. She had a tight schedule to keep, but she couldn't make herself start the engine.

There was something going on with her sister. She'd looked disheveled and bleary-eyed, and her blouse had been buttoned up wrong. Charlotte didn't want to speculate on the cause. And those phone messages she'd heard concerned her. Was Melanie considering a move to Seattle?

What Charlotte did want was to let her sister know how much she loved her. How happy she was that she'd come home, and how much she wanted her to stay. She'd hesitated telling Melanie this before, because she hadn't wanted to pressure her, but now she felt a strong urge to say all the things she'd been holding back.

Resolutely, Charlotte swung open the car door and stepped outside. She hurried up the stairs and opened Melanie's door. She started to call out, just to let her sister know she was back, when what she overheard made her blood run cold.

Melanie was standing at the kitchen counter, her back to the door, telephone pressed to her ear.

"Cocaine," her sister said, then paused a moment. "I want everything you've got. All of it."

LATER THAT AFTERNOON, back at the restaurant, Melanie was nervous. She couldn't stop thinking about what Coby had told her this morning as she flitted between tasks at Chez Remy.

Her thoughts skipped wildly as she whisked eggs for a hollandaise sauce, then promptly forgot what she was supposed to be making. She mixed ingredients for a chutney, then abandoned it to peer inside the oven, where she'd stuck a cold salad meant for the refrigerator. And then she opened the freezer to discover the casserole that was supposed to have gone into the oven.

All the while she was creating mini-disasters for herself, she kept one ear tuned, waiting for the sound of Robert's boots. When at last she heard his footfall, she clenched her hands and quickly turned her head to peer over her shoulder. Just the sight of him sent her hormones into hyperdrive.

He was staring at her, his hands held behind his back.

Her heart pounded and her knees trembled. This was crazy.

He smiled and winked.

"What?" she asked.

"I bought you a present."

"You got a present for me?" That was the last thing she'd expected.

He handed her a flat box bound with a red ribbon. Feeling self-conscious, she opened it up.

"A dream catcher." She laughed. "New Orleans style. Made with beads."

"I saw it on my way into work and I remembered you told me your recipes came to you in a dream. The chocolate turkey was such a hit, we don't want to miss out on any of your dreams. The good ones get caught in the web and the bad dreams fall away."

"Robert, that's so sweet of you." She felt her cheeks flame pink. She was touched by his gift.

"Put it to good use. Dream us up five-star menus."

"I'll put it up over my bed as soon as I get home." Nervously, she shifted her weight, almost wishing she'd never contacted Coby.

Was Robert like David? Was she making the same miserable mistake? Getting caught up in the excitement, the heady exhilaration of sexual attraction, only to find herself involved with yet another man who took drugs?

But Robert didn't look like a druggie. Not with those clear, intelligent eyes, tiger-fast reflexes and rapier-sharp memory.

If Coby's research was accurate, Robert was from old money. So what was he doing in New Orleans, working a job that earned him less than seventy grand a year? Had years of drug use caused him to run through his fortune?

But Robert had been charged with cocaine possession

more than a dozen years ago. That didn't mean he was still a user. She had smoked a little pot when she was sixteen, but she'd gotten busted and learned her lesson the hard way. She hadn't taken anything stronger than an aspirin since.

Maybe Robert had also made a youthful mistake. But whereas she'd gone before the judge, accepted the probation and served her community service, Robert's powerful aunt had pulled strings and gotten him out of trouble.

Melanie could easily forgive a youthful, one-time, peer-pressure drug use. What she couldn't excuse was the idea that he had cheated. He should have been forced to face the consequences of his actions as she had, not hidden behind the skirts of his powerful aunt.

Sugarcoat it all you want. Robert had not accepted responsibility for his actions.

But would you have if your parents hadn't made you?

She cocked her head, studying him.

Her emotions warred. She was so attracted to him, but she didn't dare make the same mistake twice. There it was, the dilemma of her life—follow her passion and risk screwing up again, or force herself to play it safe, and possibly miss out on an amazing experience.

He must have sensed her mood, because his smile disappeared and that hooded look came over his face. There it was. His darker side...tempting her. She imagined him making love to her and could almost feel his hands on her body, as hot and hungry as they'd been the night before.

How she wished there wasn't this barrier between them. That she could trust him. Could they bridge the gap? Was it even a smart thing to wish for?

If Robert did use drugs and her mother found out, she

would fire him on the spot. Anne had a very strict no-tolerance policy concerning her staff and drug use.

Melanie felt a pang in her heart. An odd pain that made no sense, and yet there it was. Wanting. Needing. Aching. She barely knew Robert, so why this profound sense of sadness at the thought of no longer having him in her life?

"I HEARD HER WITH MY OWN ears. This is exactly what Melanie said on the phone— 'Cocaine. I want everything you've got. All of it.'" Distressed, Charlotte paced the floor of her office at the Hotel Marchand. She had called an emergency meeting with Renee and Sylvie to discuss their baby sister. "And just before that there was an odd message on her answering machine from some guy telling her he'd scored her some primo stuff. Now you tell me what that suggests to you?"

Sylvie perched on the edge of an antique Queen Anne chair, worrying her beaded necklace with two fingers, while Renee stood with her back against the wall, hands clasped in front of her.

"I told you she's been acting restless lately," Charlotte fretted. "Distracted and moody. But I never imagined it was something like this."

"You could have taken her conversation out of context," Sylvie said. "You only heard her side of it."

"And you didn't hear the entire conversation," Renee pointed out.

"But you two didn't see her this morning. She looked like she'd been partying all night long." Charlotte's lips formed a hard line. She didn't want to believe it, either, but the evidence could not be dismissed. Her head throbbed from the tension and she felt as if she was coming completely unraveled. *Oh, Mellie, what have you gotten yourself into?*

Sylvie shook her head. "I still can't believe Melanie's doing drugs."

"Remember when she was arrested for smoking marijuana?" Charlotte asked. "No one wanted to believe it then, either, but it happened."

Sylvie shifted in her seat. "Yes, Mel burned a couple of doobies when she was sixteen. Smoking a little pot does not a drug addict make, and besides, that was thirteen years ago."

Charlotte's hand was shaking. Everything that had happened lately was closing in on her. Maybe she was jumping to conclusions about Melanie. Maybe she was using her little sister as a distraction to keep from focusing on the bigger issue here. That someone was trying to destroy the Hotel Marchand and she couldn't seem to stop it from happening.

Renee came over to rest a hand on Charlotte's shoulder. "You've been under so much stress. Maybe you're starting to see mountains where there are only molehills. Sylvie and I will quietly talk to Melanie and see what we can find out. You've got enough on your plate with the Charboneaux-Long wedding and Mardi Gras preparations."

"I don't think talking to her quietly will be enough," Charlotte said. "If she's using drugs, she's just going to deny it."

"Then again," Sylvie said, "we shouldn't confront her unless we have real proof. We don't want to jump the gun. But you're right, if we talk to Melanie we're probably not going to get much out of her. Why don't we ask Robert if he's noticed anything amiss? He's with her more than we are."

Charlotte took a deep breath. "You're right. I'll talk to Robert."

Even though it didn't feel like enough, it was a start.

CHAPTER NINE

THE MOOD IN THE KITCHEN had changed and Robert wasn't sure why. After he'd given Melanie the dream catcher, she'd become subdued. And she kept making mistakes with the food preparations, which wasn't like her. He put it down to the stress of the previous night. Maybe she was regretting having been so open about wanting to have sex with him. Or had she read more into the dream catcher gift than he'd intended, and it was throwing her off her game?

Realizing that the longer he was in the kitchen, the more errors she seemed to make, he decided to go check out the doorbell at the service delivery entrance to see if it was working.

But as he unscrewed the faceplate holding the buzzer in place, his mind was on Melanie.

Was she hurt because he'd turned her down last night? He kept remembering the look of sexual hunger in her eyes. What had his fear of getting hurt caused him to miss out on? She'd told him he was too controlled. She'd called him mannequin man.

Ha! If only she knew the truth.

Did she really think he was that uncaring? He sat down hard on the cold concrete steps and wished last night had never happened. It had stirred up so many unwanted feelings. Feelings that scared him, because the minute he let himself think *Maybe she's the one,* he grew terrified it would all be taken away. In his mind, love equaled loss, and try as he might, he could see no way to change his thinking.

How was he going to keep working side by side with Melanie when he had such a strong desire to take her to bed? Damn it, he'd finally found some measure of peace here in New Orleans, and now he'd gone and screwed it up.

You haven't screwed it up. As long as you don't sleep with her, everything will be okay. Just keep your distance and these feelings will pass.

"Robert?"

The sound of Charlotte's voice almost jettisoned him out of his skin. He hadn't heard her come up behind him.

"Charlotte." He hopped to his feet and stuck the screwdriver in his back pocket.

"What are you doing out here?" Charlotte had a newspaper tucked under her arm. She wore a charcoal pin-striped suit with a pink silk blouse and looked both professional and feminine.

Robert had the utmost respect for the eldest Marchand sister. In fact, the two of them were a lot alike. Both type A personalities, both efficient and devoted to their careers, both brought up in privilege.

"Door buzzer's not working. I tried to repair it myself, but I'll have to call maintenance."

"I wanted to thank you for this." She thrust the *Times-Picayune* toward him.

He glanced down and saw a photo of the Hotel Marchand with the caption: "Hotel Haunted?" The byline was by Jeri Kay Loving.

"Thank me?"

"The jig's up. She mentioned you in the article."

"Oh."

"Our reservation clerk tells me the phone has been ringing off the hook since this edition hit the stands. Our bookings are showing an increase already."

"I don't understand."

"You told the reporter about the hotel's ghost. Apparently a lot of people want to stay at a haunted hotel."

"You're kidding."

"I'm absolutely serious, Robert. How did you get the reporter to write that article?"

"She's someone I used to know in Seattle. She asked me directly about the generator failure the night of the blackout, so I told her I figured it might have something to do with the resident ghost. I never imagined she'd print it."

"Well, she did and it's a blessing."

"I'm just glad it helped. Are you any closer to finding out who did disable the generator?"

She shook her head. "No. And sometimes I wonder if we ever will. I'm almost hoping it was someone's idea of a bad joke. I can't imagine anyone wanting to harm the hotel. Fingers crossed we'll get through the rest of the Mardi Gras without any more incidents."

"If there's anything I can do…"

"There is something else that I wanted to talk to you about." Charlotte stepped closer and glanced around, presumably to see if they were alone.

Robert looked at her expectantly. Something was definitely worrying her.

"What is it?" Robert prodded.

Charlotte took a deep breath, and clasped her hands together. "Have you…" She trailed off, then started again. "Have you noticed anything different about Melanie lately?"

So that's what this was about. "What do you mean exactly?"

"Has she been late to work?"

"Once or twice."

"Forgetful?"

He shrugged, thinking of this morning. Melanie had made a mess of one dish after another.

"Slipping off on unscheduled breaks? Any unusual behavior?"

"You know Melanie," he hedged, uncertain what Charlotte was fishing for and not wanting to get Melanie into trouble with her sister. "She's a creative woman. She's hard to predict."

Charlotte cleared her throat. "Do you think she's considering leaving town? Has she said anything about a job offer? A new romance in another city?"

The idea struck him like a blow. Robert had to press his lips together to keep from wincing, and then had to ask himself why the notion bothered him so much. It wasn't as if he and Melanie were dating.

But you could be. If you wanted.

He didn't want. She deserved someone who could laugh and play with her. Not a mannequin man who had to hold on tightly to his emotions in order to battle the ghosts from his past. Not a man who had mental illness running through his DNA.

"No," he said. "She hasn't mentioned anything about moving or having a boyfriend. In fact, we've been discussing taking Chez Remy to a whole new level. Between her cooking and my management skills, I think we can make this happen."

"Really?" Charlotte sounded hopeful.

"Yes."

"So you don't think something's troubling Melanie?"

You mean besides me? "She told me she's been dreading this bachelorette auction thing, but that she's determined not to let you down."

"I see." Charlotte paused a moment, then said, "Robert, I've got a proposition for you."

ON THURSDAY NIGHT Melanie found herself standing behind the stage of the small auditorium in the Garden District pre–Civil War mansion that served as the headquarters for the New Orleans Historical Renovation Society.

Her hair was twisted up in a chic chignon and she wore Charlotte's silver formal gown, cinched almost too tightly at the waist—she should have taken her advice, Melanie admitted, tried it on and had it altered before the auction—and a silver sequined mask the event coordinator had insisted she wear. Hiding behind masks was a timeless Mardi Gras theme, but Melanie had never been much for masquerades.

Grand-mère Celeste waited in the wings with her, the knuckle of her index finger pressed to Melanie's spine to make sure she stood up straight. The silk moiré walls of the room, the Persian carpet, the gleaming cherrywood furniture, the accessories in rich neutral colors all whispered wealth and good breeding. It certainly wasn't Melanie's kind of place. Too stuffy by half. But it was part of her heritage.

Leave it to the New Orleans Ladies-Who-Lunch to go all out.

"You look beautiful." Her grandmother nodded approvingly. "Thank you for standing in for Charlotte. I'm very proud of you."

"Thanks, Grand-mère."

"It's 'thank you.' 'Thanks' is casual slang." Her grand-mother looked at her as if she'd just scored a big fat F on the elegant-lady test.

"Sorry."

"Apology accepted. Don't worry, we'll make a Robichaux of you yet," Celeste said, referring to her side of the family.

Here it was again. The feeling that she'd never really belonged in her own family. Melanie was the odd girl out. She bit the inside of her cheek to keep from retorting. Celeste was an elderly woman, after all, even if she wielded a sharp tongue.

What was it going to take for Melanie to fit in?

Maybe you never will. Maybe you should just accept it.

The ache in her heart was sharp and unexpected. Until this moment she hadn't realized exactly how much she wanted to change. She just wasn't sure where to start.

"And now for our next bachelorette," the emcee, Henry Dumas, crooned into the microphone. Henry was an old friend of Celeste's and hailed from Texas oil money.

Melanie tensed and mentally prepped herself. *Come on, you can do this.* Her chest felt tight and she drew in a deep, unsteady breath. She was more afraid of disappointing her grandmother, she realized suddenly, than of being bid on by Wilmer Haddock.

"Here is the utterly charming youngest Marchand daughter, Melanie," Henry continued. "Melanie is a sous-chef at Chez Remy. They say the way to a man's heart is through his stomach, and Melanie proves that's true. I recently was treated to a meal of her chocolate turkey and instantly fell in love."

Melanie groaned inwardly at the corniness of it all, but the crowd, most of whom had known her since she was a tomboy in pigtails, burst into refined applause. Not a catcall or two-fingered whistle in the house.

Forcing a smile that she did not feel, Melanie stepped out onto the stage. The spotlight followed her with a digitalized drumroll. She found it unnerving, gazing out into a sea of tuxedos, ball gowns and masked faces.

She felt a nervous tic at her right eye. More than anything she wished she could twitch her nose and be magically transported to her favorite place on earth—her father's kitchen.

Thinking about Chez Remy made her think about Robert, and thinking about Robert made her think about getting locked in the supply pantry with him and how he had turned down sex with her when things had gotten hot and heavy.

She honestly did not know how to read the guy. One minute he'd been kissing her like there was no tomorrow, and the next he was backpedaling and contradicting himself. Her ego wanted to believe it was because he'd been so hot for her he hadn't known how to handle it. But her insecurities were mocking her, telling her he'd just been polite, only kissing her because she'd thrown herself at him.

Oh God. She felt her cheeks flush pink remembering how foolhardy she'd been.

And then there was the bomb Coby had dropped on her about Robert's cocaine use.

It's in the past, she told herself. *It doesn't matter now.*

But did she know for certain that it *was* in the past? And even if it had happened years ago, it proved he was the kind of man who wouldn't step up to the plate and accept the consequences of his actions, but let someone else clean up his mess. Did she really want to get involved with a guy like that?

What exactly did she want from him?

"Shall we start the bidding at five hundred dollars?" Henry Dumas asked the crowd. "After all, we are talking one very hot sous-chef here."

"Five hundred," called a short, chubby balding man in a Zorro mask.

Wilmer Haddock.

Ugh.

Melanie suppressed a groan of disgust. Squinting against the glare from the overhead chandelier, she gazed out at the audience, searching for a knight in shining armor to save her from a fate worse than death—four hours in the company of Wilmer Haddock.

Double ugh.

Please, God, let someone else bid on me.

"Five hundred," Henry said. "Do I hear five-ten?"

"Six hundred," someone at the back of the room called out.

Saved! She had another bidder.

Glaring, Wilmer whipped his head around to find out who was competing against him, stated, "Seven hundred."

"A thousand." The counteroffer came promptly from the back of the room.

Now everyone was staring at the stranger.

Who was he?

Melanie stood on her tiptoes and craned to see who was giving Wilmer a run for his money. Unfortunately for her, the Haddock family had very deep pockets and Wilmer possessed a competitive streak. Even worse, she knew he'd been praying for an opportunity like this to recreate their sophomore year church picnic.

Charlotte, you owe me big for this, Melanie thought.

"Fifteen hundred," Wilmer called.

Silence fell over the room.

Oh no, was her savior dropping out? Melanie pasted a bright, encouraging smile on her face. *Don't forsake me now, Romeo.*

"Two thousand."

Melanie scanned the back of the room and finally saw who was outbidding Wilmer. A man in a tuxedo with a Phantom of the Opera mask.

Her pulse thumped. She loved the Phantom of the Opera. Dark, brooding, sexy. And this one was willing to fork out two grand to spend the evening with her.

Rock on, Phantom.

Wilmer bared his teeth. "Three thousand dollars," he exclaimed boldly, then shot a triumphant glance over his shoulder.

The audience applauded politely.

Melanie's hopes shattered.

Rats. Looked like she was in for a long night of batting Zorro away from her cleavage. Oh well, it was for a good cause. No one could say she hadn't held up her end of the bargain.

"Five," the Phantom said quietly.

"Excuse me?" Henry Dumas cupped a hand around his ear. "Didn't quite catch that. Did you say five thousand dollars for an evening with Melanie Marchand?"

"I did."

Holy cow. Five grand? Melanie felt both giddy and faint. Who was this guy?

A ripple went through the crowd. None of the previous bachelorettes had raised anything close to that extravagant amount.

Henry looked at Wilmer. "Do you want to make a counter offer?"

Wilmer opened his mouth to put in another bid, but before he could say anything, Melanie snatched the microphone from a startled Henry, not caring one whit that she was breaking all the rules of decorum, not to mention the auction.

"Going once, going twice, going three times. I'm sold to the Phantom of the Opera for five thousand dollars."

The crowd chortled.

Wilmer glared.

Henry grabbed for his microphone.

The Phantom meandered through the crowd to collect his prize.

And Melanie's heart practically jumped right out of her chest, it was beating so hard.

In his elegant, form-fitting tux, he outshone every man in the place. But it wasn't the tuxedo that lent him his powerful sexual allure. Indeed, if he'd been wearing nothing but black woolen socks he would still have overshadowed them all.

Melanie found herself trying to imagine exactly what he did look like beneath those fancy duds, and she heated from the inside out.

Everyone was staring at him—the men with envy, the women with desire. And Wilmer looked as if he wanted to take out a gun and shoot him.

Melanie would be leaving the party with this guy....

Her benefactor settled up with the event coordinator as Melanie stepped down off the stage and the next bachelorette came on to take her place.

"Lucky girl," Grand-mère Celeste said from behind her. "You ended up with the best man in the house."

Melanie looked at her grandmother. "Did you set this up?"

"Charlotte and I couldn't very well let that weaselly Wilmer Haddock win you, now could we?"

"Thank you, Grand-mère!" She turned and hugged her grandmother. "What do I do now?"

"Go have fun."

The other bachelorettes had gone with their dates to the party in the next room, where a jazz band was playing. But there was nothing in the rules of the auction that said Melanie had to stay here at the costume ball with *her* date.

The Phantom strode toward her with an air of supreme confidence. He reached her just about the time she realized she'd stopped breathing. She felt light-headed and downright giddy. And the disguise of the masks made it all the more fun.

He held out his arm.

Their eyes met.

Her stomach churned.

He smiled.

Without a word passing between them, she took his elbow. He nodded at Grand-mère Celeste. She smiled back.

The Phantom swept Melanie from the auditorium, but stopped in the corridor, inclining his head first to the ballroom and then to the exit door.

Which way? His eyes silently asked.

She met his gaze and smiled coyly. *You figure it out.*

He nodded knowingly, took her to the coat closet to claim her cloak, and then escorted her toward the exit. They stepped out into the cool night air of the courtyard, both still wearing their masks.

The minute they were on the street, she pulled away from him. "Just who are you?"

His smile was enigmatic. "Can't you guess?"

CHAPTER TEN

"ROBERT," SHE SAID and there was no missing the purr of pleasure in her voice. "It's you."

"Melanie." He grinned.

He felt like the lead in some romantic movie—tuxedos, high-society bachelorette auctions, moonlight and a beautiful woman looking at him as if he'd hung the stars in the sky just for her. It had been a very long time since he'd felt like this, and it scared him as much as it thrilled him.

"I can't believe you just did that." Playfully, Melanie swatted his arm. "Why did you do that for me?"

"I'm a sucker for a damsel in distress."

She pointed a finger at him. "You were in cahoots with Grand-mère Celeste."

"Sort of. Charlotte came to see me and told me how distressed you were over this Wilmer Haddock character bidding on you. She approached your grandmother about it, and Celeste offered to go in half with me on the charity money if I'd outbid Haddock."

"Oh, that was so sweet of Charlotte. And it was sweet of you, too, Robert. That's a sizable donation to charity, even with Grand-mère pitching in half."

"It's for a worthy cause, and the important thing is that you and I get to spend some time alone together away from the kitchen. But thank you for taking the microphone away from the emcee and ending the auction when you did."

She slid him a sidelong glance that started something unraveling inside him. "You really want to spend the evening with me?"

"Hell, yes."

"I hate to tell you, Robert, but all you had to do was ask and you could have had me for free."

"But then I wouldn't have been able to make a grand gesture, would I?"

"I suppose not."

Suddenly, Robert felt unsure of himself. He thought of his awkward teenage years, when he hadn't had a father to teach him how to behave around girls. He felt as inept now as he had then. But he'd be damned if he'd let Melanie see his vulnerability. To bolster his courage, he stepped closer, encroaching on her space, taking control. Doing the one thing that had always made him feel secure.

His plan to unsettle her so she couldn't see exactly how much she unsettled him had succeeded. Melanie took a step back and peered at him nervously. He watched the column of her throat move as she swallowed.

"So, um, what do you want to do now?"

"There's a party going on in there." He inclined his head toward the house they'd just left. "Live band, lots of food. Your grandmother pulled out all the stops."

"I don't really enjoy those uptight society events. Too much meaningless small talk."

"What do you like?"

"Let's do something fun," she said. "Something wild and

crazy in these monkey suits and masks. Something you've never done before."

"Like what?"

"I don't know. Just something unexpected."

He felt the immense pressure of wanting to please her. Of coming up with something to keep that fire sparking in her eyes. He searched his brain, but all he think of was the usual tourist stuff.

"Riverboat gambling?"

"Nah."

"Jazz club?"

"Not in the mood. Although snuggling in a darkened club does have its appeal." She flashed him an impish grin.

"I'm going to confess, it's a little hard to top wild and crazy for a woman raised in New Orleans."

"I've got it." She snapped her fingers. "There's a carnival in town set up near the pier."

"A carnival?"

"We could ride the merry-go-round. I adore merry-go-rounds. Come with me, Phantom."

She took his hand, and right then, he decided to allow her to lead him astray.

They walked the crowded streets in their finery and masks, but in a town like New Orleans they barely caused a stir. A few tourists craned their necks for a second look, but that was all. They reached the pier after a half hour stroll. The sky had darkened since they'd left the auction, and the wind had picked up, but the water was strangely calm.

The pier was strung with lights—white, red and yellow bulbs beckoning them closer. Since it was the middle of the week, the crowd was light.

They ambled past the arcade, where the carnival barkers urged them to try their luck at games of chance. Ring-toss, blow up a balloon with a water gun, and whack-a-mole. Robert hadn't been to a carnival since he was a small child. He hadn't even realized traveling carnivals like this one still existed.

Immediately to the left was a small roller coaster built to look like an elaborate mousetrap. Passengers screamed as the cars soared, then plummeted. To the right were bumper cars, and straight ahead lay the merry-go-round.

Robert bought red coupon tickets at the booth and then handed them to the ride operator. The man took down the rope and motioned for them to get on the carousel.

Twirling up onto the platform, Melanie looked like a Christmas tree angel in her silver dress, her hair twisted up in an elegant chignon. He'd never seen her so graceful and ladylike. This other side to her showed him how little he really knew about her, and anticipation grew deep inside him.

Melanie chose a bright red horse, its saucy head thrown back, mane flowing. She hiked up her skirt and swung her leg over the aging fiberglass animal. His tomboy was back in all her boisterous glory. And as much as he liked her dressed up and dazzling, he preferred the Melanie he knew best.

Robert sat down in a chariot. When the ride started, Melanie's horse soared up and down, but Robert's chariot didn't move.

"Fuddy-duddy." Melanie poked fun at him for his choice.

"This tux is a rental," he said. "I don't want to mess it up."

"A likely story. As if riding the chariot will keep your suit any cleaner than being on a horse."

"You got me," he confessed. "Although I imagine more sticky-fingered kids go for the horse than the chariot."

She looked wickedly beautiful in the gown. It clung to her curves, and her indigo eyes sparkled behind that mysterious mask. It would be so easy to fall in love with her.

Too damn easy.

"I know the real reason you won't ride the horse with me." She had to shout to be heard above the loud calliope music as they went around and around.

"Yeah?"

"It's a metaphor."

He grabbed the pole of her horse and stood up beside her so she didn't have to keep shouting at him. "A metaphor?"

"Selecting the chariot over a horse is a metaphor for everything you want to avoid." Her head bobbed up and down as, the carousel spun. "Safety over adventure, neatness over fun."

"A settled stomach over nausea."

"I suppose." She grinned. "If living life to the fullest makes you nauseous."

The merry-go-around slowed, along with the movement of her horse. The music faded.

"At least my way, when the ride is over, you don't throw up," he said.

"Maybe not. But you're left wondering if you could have enjoyed yourself more."

When the carousel came to a stop, Melanie hopped off.

"Let's get cotton candy," she said.

Without waiting for him, she took off toward the concession stand and bought blue cotton candy on a stick. She wasn't carrying a purse and had to take off her shoe to retrieve her money.

Robert shook his head. Here she was, dressed like royalty and digging money from her shoe like a kid.

Lightning flashed in the distance toward the Gulf of Mexico, followed by a hollow rumble of thunder. It was going to rain soon. He should nudge her toward home.

"Storm's coming," he said, nodding at the sky. "We should probably wrap this up."

"Mmm, wanna bite?" She peeled off a chunk of wispy blue cotton candy and offered it to him.

"No, that's okay. You go ahead."

"Your loss. It's great stuff."

"It's spun sugar and food coloring. How great can it be?"

"See there," Melanie said. "That's your basic problem. You can't enjoy something simply for the sake of enjoying it."

"What can I say? I'm driven to analyze."

"That you are."

They avoided Bourbon Street—it was always too crowded, especially as Mardi Gras approached—but the sounds of New Orleans jazz drifted into the night.

"This must have been a bizarre town to grow up in," he said. "Did you ever do the *Girls Gone Wild* thing and flash your—" his gaze fell to her cleavage and he couldn't help grinning "—um…assets for free beads?"

"That's tourist stuff. We lived here. We could get all the cheap beads we wanted. Besides, we were pretty sheltered. Catholic schools, strict curfew…"

"That explains your rebellious streak. Catholic schools. I went to them, too."

"No kidding." She eyed him coquettishly behind her mask.

"No kidding."

"But you're not rebellious."

"I guess my life was chaotic enough. I didn't have anything to rebel against. I wanted things nice and quiet."

"That explains a lot." Melanie broke off another chunk of cotton candy. "Sure you don't want a bite?"

"No, you go right ahead."

"Where to now?" she asked.

Robert glanced at the sky. "Rain's coming. Maybe we should call it a night."

"What's a little rain? Contrary to popular opinion, I don't melt when I get wet." She waved a hand at the distant lightning. "The storm is still a long ways off."

"It's almost ten—tomorrow's going to be jammed preparing for the Charboneaux-Long rehearsal dinner," he reminded her.

"If you want to blow me off, just blow me off. No need to make up excuses."

"I'm not making up excuses. There's nowhere else I'd rather be than with you."

"Really?" Her smile was genuine.

"You find it hard to believe that I want to be with you. Why's that?"

"I get this feeling you're always holding back when we're together. Is it me or is that the natural Robert?"

"I just thought that maybe you wanted out of the date."

"No way. Are you kidding? I've finally got you away from that kitchen." She reached up and traced a slightly sticky finger along his jaw. "Why don't we pretend that time has stopped? Tomorrow does not exist. Yesterday does not exist. Only now is real. Under these conditions, what would you like to do next?"

Kiss you, he thought, but said, "I am pretty tired. I got up at five-thirty this morning."

She raised a hand. "Tut, tut. This morning is in the past. It does not exist. Are you telling me you'd rather go to sleep than kiss me right here under a big cloud-shrouded moon in the French Quarter?"

It was amazing, the way she could read his mind.

"You've got your hands full of cotton candy," Robert pointed out.

She searched for a trash can, spotted one on the corner and took off at a run. Once she'd dumped the cotton candy in the trash, she raced back.

"All gone," she said breathlessly, teetering on her high heels. She puckered up and leaned toward him.

"Well, it's pretty clear what you want to do."

"Just shut up and kiss me," she said.

"And you say I'm bossy. I—"

But he didn't get to finish his sentence. She plastered her lips to his and he tasted the wonderful combination of sticky blue cotton candy and warm, moist Melanie.

He knew he was in over his head. He had known it when they were locked in the supply closet together, but he'd tried to tell himself it was nothing. This kiss refuted that argument.

A kiss wasn't just a kiss.

Not when it involved the tomboyish brunette pressed solidly against him in her silver gown.

Their masks rubbed together, making an erotic squeaking sound of plastic against plastic. The barrier should have created distance between them, but strangely enough it seemed to increase the intimacy. Their noses and foreheads and cheeks were covered, leaving only their eyes and their mouths to make contact.

They gazed into each other's eyes as their tongues dueled and their masks rubbed and their bodies sparked. He ached for her, and the sheer intensity of his aching unsettled him. Wanting her this badly made him too damn needy.

He didn't like being vulnerable. It scared him too much. Made him think about all the things he'd lost and he was tired of losing things.

Enough.

Forcibly, he tore himself away from her.

"Wow." Melanie reached up to touch her lips. "That was better than the last time."

"We shouldn't be kissing," he said. "I shouldn't be kissing you."

"Yeah? Then why did you come to the auction? Why did you bid on me?"

"I didn't want you to get stuck with someone like your friend Zorro."

"Why not?" she asked. "Why should you care?"

Robert lifted his shoulders. He didn't want to answer that question.

"Jealous maybe?" she teased.

"How can I be jealous of you?" he asked. "We're not a couple."

"No," she said. "We're not."

"Do you want to be a couple?"

"No, no." She shook her head. "Do you?"

"Not if you don't."

"But if I did, would you?"

He reached out and took her shoulders in both his hands.

Her eyelashes scraped softly against her mask when she blinked. "You already know how attracted I am to you."

"But attraction does not a relationship make."

"Right."

"I'd want to go to parties. You'd want to stay home and read. I'd want to trek in the Himalayas, climb Everest, and you'd want to stay home and organize the garage."

"You want to climb Mount Everest?"

"Figure of speech. But if the opportunity arose, I wouldn't want to miss out just because the garage needed cleaning."

"We could always cook."

"Ah, our one point of connection. Food."

"It is a strong shared value. Everyone has to eat."

They were polar opposites, but the fact remained: whenever he was with her, Robert felt more alive, more real, more like his true self than he had ever felt with anyone else.

"I know what we can do," she said. "Let's have our palms read by one of those fortune-tellers in Jackson Square. Let's go see if we're fated to be together or if we're a train wreck waiting to happen."

She took his hand and pulled him in the direction she wanted him to go.

God help him, but he felt so alive when he was with her. He didn't possess that kind of joie de vivre himself, and maybe that was why he was so attracted to people who did.

His head told him to steer clear, to shut this thing down and take her home. But his heart, his stupid, stupid heart, belonged to the ten-year-old boy he'd once been. The kid who'd had to grow up too soon because the adults in his life couldn't be trusted to be there for him.

Lightning flashed, edging closer to the city. The smell of rain was in the air.

"Have you ever had your fortune told?" Melanie asked, bumping chummily into his side as she slipped her arm through his.

They strolled down the dimly lit street just off the French Quarter, looking like prime mugging targets, he in his tuxedo, she in her designer gown.

"No," he said, keeping a firm grip on her hand. "Have you?"

"Lots of times. My father's mother used to read our palms when we were kids, although we weren't allowed to tell my grandmother Celeste about it. She didn't approve."

"Can't say as I blame her. Foretelling the future isn't exactly a wholesome childhood activity."

"My grandmother Marie died when I was six so I never got to learn the skill, although Sylvie can read palms a bit. Mostly, though, I just come to the psychics here on Jackson Square."

"Any of these psychic predictions ever come true?"

"Yeah," she answered. "A lot of them have. Even ones I wished hadn't."

He felt her exuberance drain away. Her body stiffened beside his. "Like what?"

"When I came home for Christmas four years ago, I had my palm read. The psychic told me my life was about to change forever. Two months later my father was killed on Pontchartrain Causeway."

"That was a pretty generic prediction," Robert said. "I'm not impressed."

"Trust you to rely on with your logic. You can't analyze faith, LeSoeur. You either have it or you don't."

"People's lives change forever all the time. Your father's car accident would have happened without that reading."

"But would my life have changed so dramatically? So quickly? She shuddered, and he knew she was thinking about her father. Robert was thinking about his own parents, how swiftly he'd lost them both. He'd been cheated out of a real childhood and was glad for Melanie that she'd had that. A happy childhood. A loving family.

"Are you sure you want to do this?"

"Yes." She nodded. "Things have been crappy lately, between Hurricane Katrina and Mom's heart attack. I'm due for some good fortune and I want to know it in advance."

"Come on, be serious. You don't really believe in fortune-tellers."

"Sure." She lifted a shoulder. "Why not?"

"There's no rational basis for it."

"See. That's the difference between you and me, LeSoeur. I have an open mind."

"Sometimes you need to filter things through a little common sense. Filters were made for a reason, Melanie. Keep in the good, keep out the bad."

"But how do you know what's good or bad if you're not willing to take a chance? And just because something might initially look bad doesn't mean that it isn't the best thing that could have happened in the long run."

"Let's just agree to disagree on this."

"But you'll do it with me anyway, won't you?" She looked up at him through her silver sequined mask. "Have your palm read, please, for me."

How could he turn down such a plea? "All right."

She grinned and his heart felt toasty.

They arrived in Jackson Square, and the kooks and weirdos were out in full force. Fortune-tellers and palm readers and psychics of all flavors and varieties had card tables—decorated garishly with vivid tablecloths and occult symbols—set up around the square.

"Which one do we pick?" he asked.

"Madam Lava," Melanie said with certainty. "She's supposed to be the best."

Madam Lava was set up on the north side of the square. She was a tiny shriveled woman in a purple fedora and a crimson serape. Tarot cards were spread out on the table in front of her and she had a crystal ball. When they approached, her wrinkled face dissolved into a smile as if she had been sitting there waiting just for them.

"Ah," she said in a wizened little voice that made Robert think of Yoda. "Revellers out for a bit of late night fun."

That wasn't too hard to figure out between their fancy clothes and masks.

"Who's going to be first?" Madam Lava shot Melanie a sidelong glance.

Melanie pointed at Robert. "Do him."

Robert couldn't really say why the thought of having his fortune told made him so uncomfortable, but it did.

"Have a seat, young man," Madam Lava directed.

Feeling like a dolt, he sat.

"Twenty dollars, please."

He fished a twenty from his wallet and passed it to her. She tucked it quickly and efficiently into her cleavage.

"What would you like? Tea leaves? Crystal ball? The tarot?"

"Palm reading," Melanie said. "He wants a palm reading."

Madam Lava stared at Melanie until she actually

seemed to shrink a bit, then the fortune-teller returned her attention to Robert.

"Palm reading," he confirmed.

The woman swept aside the crystal ball and tarot cards. "Now…" She closed her eyes and held out both hands, palms up. "Give me your hand."

Reluctantly, he placed his right hand in hers.

"How can she see with her eyes closed?" he whispered in an aside to Melanie, who hovered at his elbow.

"Madam Lava sees with the inner eye," the elderly lady snapped. "Now be quiet so I can do this properly."

"Yes, ma'am," he said, chastened. She could give the nuns at Saint Jerome's a run for their money.

"Hmm," she said. "I see much water. You come from a watery place."

True enough.

"And you have a sad heart," she continued. "But not for long. Great happiness is around the corner."

"That's good news."

"Your true love is not far away from you."

Involuntarily, Robert turned to look at Melanie.

"But first there will be pain. It is unavoidable."

Robert laughed.

Madam Lava's eyes flew open. "You think this is funny? You think I'm a joke."

"No, not at all."

"Do not laugh at me."

"No, sorry." He forced himself to stop laughing.

"One last word of warning," she said.

"What's that?"

"Fire. Beware of fire."

"Do you mean a literal fire or the fire of passion, heat, desire?"

She looked at him as if he was an imbecile, and waved him away. "Pah, I waste my time with you. Be gone."

Robert got up and let Melanie take his seat, wondering if he should demand a refund. She gave him a searing look and he decided against it.

"What?" he asked when she continued to glare at him.

"Take off," Melanie ordered. "I don't want your negative vibes gumming up my reading."

"Oh, so that's how it is?"

"Yeah!" Melanie shooed him away but she was grinning, letting him know she didn't take the reading all that seriously, either.

He walked over and sat on the nearby stone wall that encircled Jackson Square, waiting while Melanie had her reading. The wind had shifted, blowing the storm closer. Very soon it would start raining.

He liked Melanie a lot. His heart responded when she called to him, challenging him to come out and play. But his wearisome, practical head kept whispering things like *great passion leads to a great fall.*

It was only then that he realized he was still wearing his Phantom of the Opera get-up.

He pulled the mask off and took a deep breath. Weirdly, it felt as if the thing was still on his face because he'd worn it for so long. He watched Melanie sitting at the card table, looking earnestly into Madam Lava's face, hanging on the woman's every word.

Melanie sat tall and erect, a determined set to her chin.

He liked the way she challenged him, made him rethink his position on things, reevaluate his beliefs.

And that was the beginning of his knowing. He wanted her for his own, but had no clue how to make that happen.

MELANIE DIDN'T REALLY know why she was doing this. It suddenly felt pointless and silly as she sat across from the fortune-teller, her palm held up for Madam Lava's scrutiny. The woman's fingernails were long and yellowed, and the skin along her neck looked like crepe. She smelled of menthol cigarettes and cheap bourbon.

"You've been on a long journey back home," Madam Lava began once Melanie had loosened her lips with a twenty dollar bill.

"In a manner of speaking, I suppose you could say that's true," she replied.

"I see much love all around you."

Love. That was good. Her family did love her. She'd never doubted that.

"But beware," Madam Lava said. "Much trouble lies ahead."

Melanie groaned. She'd started this mess, but the last thing she wanted was a spooky fortune. She wanted Madam Lava to tell her that her future was so bright she should buy stock in designer sunshades. The fortune-teller, however, was not cooperating.

The woman squinted at Melanie's palm. "Beware of your heart. It is in grave danger."

"You might be right on that score," Melanie joked to dispel the uneasiness stealing over her. "I do tend to eat a lot of butter. I know it's not good for you but I can't help myself. You see, I'm a chef, and nothing cuts it quite like butter."

"You purposely misunderstand me." Madam Lava lifted her head and cast a dark glance at Robert, sitting on the wall a few feet away from them.

Nervously, Melanie jiggled her leg. The old woman seemed to know exactly the effect she was having on her. Was this a ploy to milk more money out of her?

"Just to let you know, I won't pay more for a better fortune."

"This is not about money. Listen carefully. This is for your own good. I'm telling you to beware." The old woman was still staring intently at Robert.

"Him? You're saying Robert is the grave danger to my heart? Oh no. You've got that all wrong. We're just coworkers. Friends." Who was she trying to kid? The fortune-teller or herself?

"Beware," Madam Lava repeated. She was beginning to sound like Poe's raven with its "nevermore."

"Okay, I get it. Beware." Melanie pulled her hand away from the fortune-teller. On wobbly legs she pushed back from the card table and stood up with a muttered thanks.

Robert dropped down off the wall and came over to link his arm through hers. "How'd it go?" he asked.

"Nevermore," she croaked, and laughed when he gave her a funny look.

"What does that mean?"

Her heart quivered strangely when she looked at him, but she pretended not to notice. "It means you're right and I'm wrong. Palm reading is silly."

"What did she say to you?"

"It was nothing. Not important."

Lightning forked. Thunder grumbled. Fat drops of rain fell from the sky.

The fortune-tellers on the square began to gather their belongings, closing up shop.

"Let's get you home," Robert said. "My car's parked near the Historical Restoration Society."

He slipped his arm around hers, and as they hurried off into the quickening rain, Melanie heard Madam Lava whisper, "Beware."

CHAPTER ELEVEN

BY THE TIME THEY REACHED her apartment, the rain was coming down so hard they could barely see through the windshield. Robert had a tarp in his car—trust him to be prepared for anything—and he held it over their heads as they ran for the door.

Rain sluicing off the tarp, they stood on the landing as Melanie lifted up the welcome mat and retrieved her house key.

"That's extremely foolhardy," Robert said. "Leaving your key under the welcome mat."

"I don't like to carry a purse," she said.

"You need to install an alarm system. That way you can just punch in a code."

"I don't know how long I'm going to live here. I see no point in investing money into a security system when I'm just going to move."

"Do you move a lot?"

"I have," she admitted.

"Why?"

"I get edgy staying in one place."

"But you're home now."

Was she? Melanie wasn't sure of that.

She let them into her apartment, turned on the light and tossed her key onto the table. The little black kitten ran up to greet them, rubbing her small dark head against Melanie's ankle and purring loudly.

"You have a cat. I didn't know you had a cat." Robert bent down to tickle the kitten under her chin.

"You like cats?"

"They're quiet, clean and mysterious. What's not to like? Is it a boy or a girl?"

"Girl."

"What's her name?"

"Um…she doesn't have one. She's not really my cat. She showed up one night, hungry and skinny-looking, so I fed her. But she's not mine."

"Aha," Robert said. "It all makes sense now."

"What does?"

"You're Holly Golightly."

"Who?"

"From *Breakfast at Tiffany's*. Audrey Hepburn. You remember, she has a cat but refuses to name it because if she named it it would belong to her, and she's so scared of being responsible for something that she can't even commit to a pet. But the very thing she's running from is the thing she needs most."

"Are you saying I'm a commitmentphobe?"

"All I'm saying is that you haven't named your cat."

"She's not my cat and I'm not commitmentphobic. I've been married."

"And divorced."

"There was a good reason for that."

Robert waved at her bare walls, at the packing boxes stacked in one corner. "You've lived here how long? Four months? No pictures on the walls, boxes still not unpacked from your move. A cat with no name. It adds up."

"How do you know those boxes are from my move? Maybe I'm getting ready to ship something."

"Because the contents are marked." He tilted his head as he read. "Household. Knickknacks. David's stuff." He looked at her. "David's stuff?"

"My ex-husband. A box his of things got mixed up with mine when I moved, and even after all this time, I've been reluctant to contact him about returning it. Hey, who wants to open that can of worms? Although if I was being a truly witchy ex-wife I would just throw it away."

"You wouldn't."

"How do you know?"

"You're not the vindictive type."

Melanie eyed him. "Hey, your tuxedo is soaking wet. Maybe there's something in there you can wear."

She dug through the box and found a pair of worn blue jeans and a T-shirt advertising Maine lobsters. She tossed them at him. "These should fit. You change in the bathroom, I'll go to my bedroom and do the Cinderella at midnight thing and get out of this ball gown."

"I don't like the idea of wearing your ex-husband's clothes," Robert said.

"You like the idea of sitting around in a wet tuxedo better? Yes, David was a jerk, but you're not going to catch mutant genes from his clothes."

"I should probably just go." Robert turned toward the door.

"Don't be absurd. It's torrential out there and you live all the way across town." To underscore her statement, a loud clap of thunder shook the building and the wind gusted loudly.

She swished to the bathroom in her rain-soaked taffeta, stripped it off and then shimmied into a pair of old workout clothes that had been relegated to pajama duty, and went back to the kitchen.

She met Robert in the hallway as he was coming from the bathroom. She whistled. "Hey, you look a hell of a lot better in those jeans than David ever did. Anyone ever tell you what a fine butt you have, LeSoeur?"

"Actually, I have been paid that compliment a time or two."

"Oh, really? I'm not the first gal to lust after your backside then?"

"Yep, there's been backside lust before you."

"I think I'm jealous."

Their eyes met and they grinned at each other.

"You want a glass of wine?" she asked. "I've got some chardonnay in the fridge."

"I really should be going."

"Come on. Wait out the storm."

"I've driven in storms before."

"I'd feel terrible if you had an accident. Please, stay. If wine's not to your liking I think there's some rum in the cabinet. Want a rum and cola?"

She thought he was going to turn her down, and she really didn't want him to go. Suddenly she hated the idea of being alone on a stormy night.

Something in her face must have given her away, because Robert relented. "I suppose I could stay for one drink, and then, to be on the safe side, take a taxi home."

"Go if you want to go," she said perversely. "I don't need a pity drink."

"It's not a pity drink."

"What is it then?"

"Maybe I don't want to leave yet."

"You were raring to run out of here just minutes ago. What changed your mind?"

"I got to thinking maybe you were afraid of storms and needed some company."

"Or," she said, "maybe you're the one who's afraid of storms. I saw the way you were gripping that steering wheel on the way over here."

"Maybe I am a little, but you know what I'm really afraid of?"

"What's that?"

"Mixing you with alcohol." He leaned against the wall between the kitchen and her living room.

"What do you mean by that?" She breezed past him to retrieve the rum from the cupboard, her shoulder brushing against his. Goose bumps tripped up her arm, hot and exciting as lightning.

"I mean that when I'm around you, my resistance is already lowered. Throw alcohol into the mix and I'm not sure I can be held responsible for my actions."

Me either, she thought, but said, "Is that a threat or a promise?"

"Are you toying with me?"

"What do you think?"

"I think you look damn hot in those stretchy workout pants, and I'm in too deep."

"And that's a bad thing?"

She passed by him again, this time purposely making sure she did not touch him. She didn't trust herself not to rip off his clothes if that happened. Especially when he was flashing those dimples her way.

She got a can of cola from the fridge and popped the pull top. The rum was for cooking, so it wasn't the highest quality, but she hoped it tasted all right. She poured the rum and cola into two tumblers, added a couple of cubes of ice and passed him one of the drinks.

Melanie raised her glass. "Cheers. If there ever was a man who needed his resistance lowered, it's you, Robert LeSoeur. You're wound way too tightly."

"And you're just the woman to unwind me?"

"Hey, everyone's got a talent. Resistance lowering just happens to be mine."

"Cheers." He clinked his glass against hers and they both took a drink. "Here's to you."

"Let's do something," she said as the hot rush of rum went to her head. She needed to move in order to cover up her nervousness. She was terrified Robert would discover she was a lot more talk than action.

"Do something?" He looked as stricken as if she'd suggested he perform an impromptu striptease.

"I'll put on some music and we can dance."

"I don't dance."

"Of course you don't. All that upright resistance. I should have known."

The kitten wandered over, and to hide her disappointment, Melanie picked her up and slowly began stroking her ears. She went to the stereo system in the corner of the adjoining living room and put on a Faith Hill CD.

"It's why we would never work as a couple—you don't and I do," she babbled, not even knowing what she was saying. Just talking to fill the air.

Kiss me, she thought. *Kiss me and make me stop talking.*

He stepped closer, eyelids half-closed, voice husky. "Do what?"

"Do anything."

"Exactly what *have* you done?"

"You'll need to be more specific."

"Ever had a one-night stand?" he asked, but then hurriedly added, "Never mind. I really don't want to know the answer."

"Don't worry." She smiled smugly. "I'm not the type to kiss and tell."

He raised his palms. "Enough said."

"You?"

"Me what?"

"Have you ever had a one-night stand?"

"No."

"You ever been married?"

"Almost."

"What happened?"

She saw him reach up and touch his temple, rub that old scar. "Let's just say we were too much alike." He said it coolly, but the look on his face told her that the failed relationship wasn't responsible for the sadness he carried within him.

"I'm sorry to hear it."

"Well, you know. That's life. Like you and what's-his-face."

"David."

"Yeah, him. How long were you married?"

"Four months. But I married him after only knowing him

a few weeks. It was one of those stupid, impulsive things. What can I say? Everyone does something really stupid at least once in their life. David was my one really stupid thing."

This was the perfect opportunity for a little quid pro quo, she realized. To see if he would come clean about his cocaine possession charges. She took a deep breath.

"Have you ever done anything really stupid?" she asked. "Something you totally regretted?"

He shook his head. "I have a lot of regrets but I don't know if you'd call any of them really stupid. *Misguided* might be a better word."

"You ever been arrested?" she asked, keeping her eyes trained on his face as she searched for a reaction.

He hesitated for a fraction of a second. "No."

Melanie saw nothing in his expression that gave away his secret, nothing that said, *Hey, I'm a big fat liar.* She shifted uncomfortably, suddenly feeling ill at ease. He was a very good liar and that was a very bad thing.

"Have you?" Robert met her gaze and held it, unblinking.

"Actually, yes."

That's when she got a reaction. He looked shocked. "What did you do?"

"Got busted for smoking a joint at a party when I was sixteen." She held his eyes, taking his measure.

Say something. Tell me you got busted for cocaine. Show me we have something in common. That we both screwed up when we were young and we regret the hell out of it.

But he didn't say anthing.

"My parents, especially my mother, knew people in high places. They could have had the charges expunged." She waited. *Tell me about your aunt. Say something!*

"They didn't?"

"No." *Not like your aunt did for you.* "They understood the importance of making me face the consequences of my actions. I served eighty hours of community service and I had to pay a fine that was more than my yearly allowance. I was sentenced to kitchen duty at Chez Remy as part of my punishment. It was the best thing my parents ever did for me."

"You haven't done drugs since then?" he asked.

"No, sir. I was scared straight."

He looked at her as if he wanted to believe her, but just couldn't. What was with him? He was the one who was holding out. She'd come clean. She'd smacked all her cards down on the table faceup for all to see, and Mr. Sphinx here wasn't sharing a thing. So much for getting up close and personal.

She took one last stab at it. "Have you ever done drugs?"

"No."

"Not once? Not ever? Not even when you were young and going through an experimental phase?"

"Never," he said. There was an emotional timbre in his voice that snagged her attention, but she couldn't get a read on exactly what the emotion was. Guilt? Regret? Sadness? "Drugs can do terrible things to people."

Merciless disappointment stole over her. Robert was lying to her. She was having such a hard time with him. How could she ever really trust Robert if he couldn't tell her the truth about himself?

"We have the oddest conversations," he said. "Have you ever noticed that? They're circular. They don't really seem to go anywhere. What's that about?"

"One person's odd is another person's normal. Besides, I believe the best conversation aren't linear discussions that come to simple conclusions. Really good conversations evolve, rise and fall, change tones and tempos."

"So who's the normal one here?" he asked. "Me or you?"

"Definitely you."

"Funny. I always thought of myself as the odd man out. Growing up, I spent a lot of time alone."

She stared at him. "You ate a lot of TV dinners as a kid, didn't you?"

He looked taken aback. "How did you know?"

"It's obvious. They warped you for life. You've got that frozen-drumstick-and-instant-mashed-potatoes look about you that time can't erase." Her tone was teasing.

"That doesn't make any sense."

"Did I call it or not?"

"That you did. So now you know my dirty little secret. I grew up a rich kid in a poor home."

"What do you mean by that?"

"My family had money. Lots of it. Even before they died I didn't spend much time with my parents. My father was into making money and my mother had her own problems. The housekeeper microwaved my dinners from a cardboard carton." Robert polished off his drink with one long swallow.

Not wanting to be left out, Melanie finished hers, too.

"Poor kid." She reached out and touched his arm, sorry for teasing him.

"Poor little rich kid, boo-hoo."

"A legacy of TV dinners explains why you're a chef."

"It does?"

"You hunger for the cozy warmth of a real kitchen, but you're still so famished inside. You should let me make it up to you. I'll cook you fried chicken from scratch."

"That's the ticket," he said. "Homemade fried chicken would solve all my problems."

Melanie canted her head. "What are your problems, Robert? You seem pretty balanced to me. Other than being scarred for life by an excess of TV dinners."

Even though she knew she was being dramatic, she could just see him sitting in the dark, an eight-year-old kid, eating a TV dinner of soggy enchiladas and cherry pie with no cherries in it, while watching reruns of The Waltons, wishing he had a family like that. She'd had such a family—loving, loyal, close-knit—and she'd so underappreciated them.

"You." He stepped closer.

The kitten jumped out of her arms and trotted off on a mission of her own.

"Me? What about me?"

"You're my biggest problem," he said.

"How's that? I undermine your authority on the job?"

"There is that." He moved nearer. She didn't back up. "But that wasn't what I was thinking about."

"What were you thinking about?"

"You push me out of my comfort zone."

"That's a good thing. Right?"

"Except maybe I like my comfort zone."

"Maybe you don't and you don't even know that you don't," she suggested.

One step, two, three and then he was right in front of her nose.

"Does this feel comfortable?"

No way was she going to admit that he was in her space, pushing her out of *her* comfort zone.

"Um, sure."

"Liar."

"One person's comfort is another person's misery."

"Potato, patato."

"Does anyone really say patato? Personally," she said, "I've always been partial to 'tater' myself. Or if I'm feeling spunky, there's always 'spud.'"

"So what you're saying is that there's an infinite number of ways for us to miscommunicate."

"Exactly."

"It's a wonder we manage to understand each other at all." His breath tickled her cheek.

"A miracle, really." Now she was eyeing his lips. They were incredibly close. If she moved forward a half inch, their mouths would touch.

"I read where eighty percent of communication is nonverbal," he said.

"Really? That much. Explains why the potato-patato issue isn't more of a barrier."

"Yeah. You don't have to say a thing. Cut 'em up, fry 'em in oil and everyone knows what a French fry is. It's the universal language of love."

"Are you saying I'm a French fry?" she asked.

"I'm saying that you're much tastier than a French fry."

Neither of them said anything, and it was all nonverbal communication from then on out.

Robert splayed his palm against the back of her head and pulled her close for a kiss so savage Melanie couldn't think beyond *More, more, gotta have more.*

And then she couldn't even think at all.

Robert's mouth branded her hotly, completely, and she relished it to her core. There was something positive to be said, after all, for bossy, take-charge men.

He tasted like rum and Coca-Cola and smelled like a cross between spray starch and designer cologne. He snaked an arm around her waist and pulled her up tighter against him.

It was late and they'd both had rum and cola and there was soft music playing and he'd outbid Wilmer Haddock for the pleasure of her company. All heady stuff.

Plus, the man was one hell of a kisser.

Who could fight that?

He pulled his mouth from hers and then very gently set her aside. "I better go."

"You could stay the night. It's still raining and you've been drinking. Sure, you could call a cab, but then your car would still be here."

"I don't think staying overnight would be such a hot idea." He edged closer toward the door.

"Why not?"

"I don't think either one of us is ready for this step in our relationship."

"Who said anything about a relationship?" she said, more to protect her ego than anything else. "I just asked you to spend the night. I never said a word about spending it in my bed. The couch folds out."

"Oh." He had the good grace to look embarrassed. "My misunderstanding."

She felt weird about this whole thing. Should she grab him by the collar and drag him to bed like a cave woman? Or back off and give him the space he needed to digest what was going down between them?

She cast a sideways glance at him and was surprised to find him looking at her with a strange sense of wonder.

It felt as if there were a thin, but incredibly strong thread—

something like a spider's web—stretching from his solar plexus straight into hers. They were standing between the lit kitchen and the dark living room, their faces half in light, half in shadows.

In that pause between heartbeats, she could see all the way into him, or at least fancied that she could, and that he could see into her. Unexpectedly, trust rose in that short span of space, in that whisper of silence.

But if she blinked, would the moment be over? Was their silence the only thing keeping this instant in perfect harmony? They kept staring at each other in a confusing mixture of admiration, consternation and sexual arousal.

She held her breath, waiting for what was going to happen next.

He moved close to her again, spanning the distance in one long step. But then he stopped short, his eyes never leaving her face.

Oh, boy. She realized they both knew that they were going to cause each other equal parts pleasure and misery.

"Lucky for you," he said, his voice thick and sultry as he raised his palms up to her, "I've got big hands."

Her heart hopped backward to bump against her spine.

At last, she thought, *a man who can handle me, but who knows how to do it gently.*

"Got sheets?"

"What?" She blinked, pulled from her dazed thoughts.

"For the fold-out couch." He gestured toward her sofa with one of those big hands.

He was so near she could feel the warmth of his skin, and she wanted him to kiss her again but was too afraid to ask. She wasn't afraid of what he would do, but of herself. Terrified she would strip those jeans off his body and have her way with him on the living room rug.

"Uh-huh," she said, but, spellbound by him, did not make a move.

"If you tell me where they are, I'll get them."

"No, um, I'll do it."

Forcing herself to stop looking at him, she scurried to the hallway closet where she kept the bed linens, and pulled out sheets, blankets and a pillow and brought them back to him.

"Thanks." His smile was golden. "Just to let you know, I'm an early riser—5:30 a.m."

"You won't get much sleep." She looked at the clock. "It's almost midnight."

"I like strong coffee first thing. You got any on hand?"

"Me, too. I'm not human before my second cup."

"Who gets the bathroom first? Me or you?"

"I take longer. You go first."

"Sounds like a plan."

Their eyes met.

His chest heaved.

Hers did, too.

He hardened his jaw.

She clenched her fists.

Both of them were struggling to hang on to some small measure of control, and failing spectacularly.

"We're not going to make it through the night," Robert murmured.

"No," she agreed.

He stepped toward her.

A thousand tiny needle pricks hot-wired a message to her brain. He reached out, wrapped his hands around her wrists and purposefully drew her toward him. He yanked her up flush against his chest, his gaze never leaving hers.

"You smell so good." His voice rumbled as deep as the thunder outside her door.

She was a goner, all her plans vaporized by a sexual chemistry so startling it left her breathless. She wanted him and she didn't care about anything else.

His knuckles grazed her breast as he slid his hand to the right side of her waist, and then lower to cup her buttocks in his big palm.

She gasped at his touch. His chest rubbed provocatively against hers, making Melanie even more aware of his incredibly hard muscles.

He kissed her, and she felt alive and tingling in all the right places. And then his other hand went to the left side of her waist, his fingers pressing against the scarred flesh beneath her shirt.

Robert pulled back, breaking their kiss, and his eyes widened.

Self-consciousness derailed her desires, and Melanie hitched in a breath.

He moved to lift her shirt.

She grabbed his wrist. "Don't. Please don't do that."

"Why not? I want to see you. All of you."

"I…" she moistened her lips. "I'm afraid you won't find me attractive anymore."

"Shh, don't be afraid. I won't judge you." He said that now, but he hadn't yet seen the scar.

"I'm ashamed," she whispered.

"There's nothing about your body to be ashamed of. Why are you?"

She shrugged. How to explain to him that she felt responsible for what had happened to her because she'd made a poor choice in marrying David? Her knees trembled.

"Let me see."

She shook her head.

"Melanie," Robert crooned, cupping his fingers under her chin and raising her face. "Look at me."

She looked him in the eyes.

"I know," he said.

"Know what?"

"What it's like to hurt that way. Trust me."

"You're asking a lot from me. Trusting the wrong person was how I ended up this way."

"I won't hurt you."

"I barely know you."

"You can't deny there's something between us. And I think we both know it's more than just sex. Trust me."

The need to trust him was so strong she could barely fight it. But she'd never been able to rely on her impulses. They always seemed to lead her in the wrong direction.

"You're the first," she blurted, losing her battle with caution.

"The first?" He arched an eyebrow.

"The first man I've been with since the divorce."

"How long ago was that?"

She gulped. Emotions crowded in on her. Guilt, nervousness, expectation. The need to talk and the fear that if she did talk she would chase him off.

"Four years."

"You haven't had sex in four years?"

She shook her head.

"Because of this?" His palm was flush against her waist.

She nodded.

"What happened?"

"I…I don't like to talk about it."

He made a noise of empathy, not pity. He went to raise her shirt again and this time she did not stop him. She watched his face, searching for any sign of disgust or revulsion, but saw only tenderness in his eyes. He dropped to his knees and pressed his lips sweetly against her scar, accepting her for who she was—flaws, imperfections and all.

Raising his head, he looked up at her, the scar at his temple glistening whitely in the lamplight.

"You tell me about your scar," he coaxed, reaching up to finger his temple, "and I'll tell you about mine."

CHAPTER TWELVE

THIS WAS MORE DIFFICULT than he thought. Robert had never opened up about his past the way he'd promised to open up to Melanie. Only his Aunt Pamela knew the true story of his scar.

He gritted his teeth. Talking about his past didn't come easy. Yes, it was difficult, but Melanie was worth it. He wanted her desperately, and until tonight he hadn't realized exactly how much.

He led her to the couch and sat her down beside him. She tucked her long legs underneath her, studying his face curiously in the light.

"This is hard for you," she said, seeming to understand all the emotions teeming inside him.

"Yeah," he admitted.

"You don't have to do it."

His hand went to her waist. "Yes, I do."

"I'll go first," she said. Funny, how she was rushing in to protect him from himself.

He might be a lot of things, but he wasn't a coward. "It's all right. I can do it."

"No, I'd rather go first. In case…" She trailed off.

"In case what?"

"In case you're disappointed in me."

"Melanie, what is this guilt you're carrying around with you? Why are you punishing yourself this way?"

She inhaled sharply. "I suppose it's because deep down inside I feel like I've done something wrong."

"In what way?"

"By being so impulsive. By marrying David too soon. Before I really knew him."

Robert looked into her eyes as far as he could see. "Tell me."

"David had a drug problem that I knew nothing about."

Robert's stomach tensed. He could relate so well to what she'd gone through. Caring about people so much that you didn't know what to do when they turned up with a problem too big for either of you to handle.

"We were working a lot of hours," she said, restlessly toying with a strand of hair that had fallen from the elegant chignon. No wonder she reminded him of Holly Golightly. "Trying to get our own restaurant off the ground. You know how hard that is. Especially in a city as competitive as Boston."

Robert nodded. He did indeed understand the pressure she'd been under.

"David seemed to be able to just go and go and go. I didn't understand why until I caught him in the bathroom with my compact mirror and a straw."

That old dark feeling stole over Robert. Melanie had been through the exact same thing he'd been through. He felt his connection to her deepen, felt the tentative bond between them solidify.

"He told me it was the first time. Promised it was the only time, and I was foolish enough to believe him."

"Drugs," Robert said. "The great deceiver."

She gave him a strange look he did not understand, and he felt the bond grow shaky again. What had he said to upset her?

"David kept using, of course. He grew short-tempered, seemed to be angry all the time. He started berating me on the job. Finally it got to the point where I couldn't stand working with him any longer. I told him for the sake of the marriage that I wanted out of the restaurant."

She paused and swallowed hard. Robert sensed that she had yet to reveal the most difficult part of her story.

"He shoved me. It was the first time he'd been physically abusive. I fell against the stove. The gas burner was turned on."

"Melanie." Robert heard his own pain in his voice as he breathed her name.

"I'll always bear his brand." She touched her left side.

Adrenaline surged through Robert. If her ex-husband had been in the room with them, he would have beaten the guy senseless for hurting her.

"My friend Coby took me to the hospital. They treated me for the burn, but since it was so late they kept me overnight for observation. The next morning I went home, packed my things and moved out. I filed for divorce that same afternoon."

"Good for you." She'd been smarter than him. Once things had turned violent, she'd gotten out. She was braver than him, too.

Melanie shrugged. "Turns out leaving David was the best thing I could have done for him, too. He got into rehab and turned his life around." She laughed mirthlessly. "I heard he's married again, has a baby and from all accounts is totally drug free. I'm happy for him, really I am, but I'm jealous, too. Why couldn't he have gotten clean and sober for me?"

"You just weren't meant to be with him."

"Maybe I'm not meant to be with anyone."

Robert took her hand, lifted it to his lips and softly kissed her knuckles. "Stop blaming yourself. It's not your fault. None of it was your fault. He was the addict. It was his problem, not yours."

"I jumped into marriage without looking. Everyone told me not to do it, but I was stubborn, determined to do things my own way. I married him anyway and I paid the price."

"You made a mistake. That's how we learn. Next time you'll know better."

She gave him an odd look. "I'm not sure there's going to be a next time."

"What are you saying? That you never want to get married again?"

"I don't know. I'm scared."

"We're all scared, Melanie, and scarred in some way. You and I just happen to have the physical scars to prove it."

Robert had one arm slung over the back of the couch, and she leaned closer, resting her head on his forearm and gazing up at him expectantly. His heart missed a beat or two. Those indigo eyes of hers could melt a glacier, and he'd been cold for far too long. Just being here with her lit him from the inside out. Warmed his tired soul.

She raised her hand, traced her fingers along his temple. "A knife?"

"Razor blade."

She winced. "How?"

He swallowed, unable to go on. "I'm sorry. I thought I could do this, but I just can't."

"It was that bad?"

"Worse than you can imagine." He saw her trying to guess what had happened, but knew there was no way she could.

"It's okay. It's all right. You don't have to tell me. Clearly, it's too painful for you to share." He heard the compassion in her voice, saw tears glistening in her eyes.

But he wanted to tell her. He really did. He just didn't know how to begin. How to form the words and force them from his mouth. *I, too, was betrayed by someone I loved. I understand what you went through.*

"What a pair we are." She laughed shakily. "Both battle scarred and wary, but ready to take it on the chin and try again."

The sound of her hopeful laughter struck a deep yearning within him.

"I'm glad you stayed," she said. "It feels good not to be alone."

Something tightened Robert's chest. He was trying to decide if he should go through with this or run straight out her door before he got caught any deeper in the quicksand of her eyes.

Too late.

She zapped him with another one of her meaningful stares and he felt as if a cop had taken a stun gun to his heart.

Take that and that and that, her eyes proclaimed.

"I should go," he said. "The way we're feeling, I'm afraid we're going to do something we'll both regret."

"But maybe that's exactly what we should do to chase away our ghosts." Audibly, Melanie sucked in a breath. "I want you, Robert. I've wanted you for months, and ever since we tussled over the turkey and ended up on the floor together, I've known exactly how much I want you."

"Melanie…I—"

She interrupted him, reaching up to touch his scar again. "I'm going out on a limb here—"

"I don't want you to have unrealistic expectations. I'm not sure I can—"

"I haven't felt this way about anybody in a very long—"

"—promise you anything more than good sex."

Oh, God.

All of his feelings for her—the craving, the guilt, the sadness, the desire, and the fear that he'd screw things up with her—whirled together inside him in a thick black cyclone of emotions.

"Good sex is enough," she whispered. "It doesn't have to mean anything more than that."

Robert kissed her. He had no choice. He was swept up in the brightness of her blue eyes, the fullness of her lush lips and the aching need in him that had gone unfulfilled for so long. This might be the stupidest thing he'd ever done, but his body was hell-bent on doing it.

If he kissed her, he didn't have to talk about the past, didn't have to relive the sorrow and the betrayal. Didn't have to dwell in the darkness that had dogged him most of his life. She was sweet salve to his lonely soul.

Melanie clung to him, needing him as much as he needed her. She matched the fury of his kisses, the fierceness of his welcome. They were starving for contact, hungry for connection and mad with passion for each other.

He'd been fighting his desire for her for so long. He simply couldn't fight anymore.

Both hands snug around her waist, he pulled her into his lap so that she was straddling him on the couch.

Dear Lord, he had wanted her since the first moment he'd

seen her waltz into Chez Remy with her ponytail swishing and a bewitching smile on her lips. He'd had no idea she harbored a secret pain to rival his own.

He thought about what she'd been through with her ex-husband, and immediately felt like a snake in the grass. This was a bad idea. He knew it was, but he no longer possessed the power to stop himself. He had to have this. Had to have her.

She seemed to need him just as much.

Melanie was touching him all over, thrusting her fingers through his hair while her eager mouth explored his face as if she couldn't get enough of the taste of him.

She wriggled in his lap, captured his lips with hers and inhaled him. She was so hot.

"This is a very dumb thing to do," he muttered against her lips, needing to say the words even though it was too late for either of them to stop. This moment had been a long time building. They'd crossed an invisible threshold, and retreat was next to impossible.

"Sometimes being dumb is the smartest thing you can do," she said.

That made no sense at all, but at this point, he pretended her words were pearls of rare wisdom. They could worry about the consequences later, when their judgment wasn't glazed with the bright sheen of lust.

Robert felt remorseful, but he made a choice to live with the guilt and just let himself go. He tipped right over the edge of stupidity and allowed it to take him under. Drowning his common sense, drowning his fear and his restraint.

Very quickly he stopped feeling guilty and just let the sensations come.

The next thing he knew they were in her bedroom, kicking

aside her dumbbells, throwing clothes off the bedspread. They were both naked and he wasn't sure how they'd gotten that way or how he was going to survive what he knew would happen next.

"Hey," he said. "You put up the dream catcher."

"But of course. It was a gift."

He kissed her again. Long and hard.

"You sure you want to do this?" The last thing he wanted was for her to have regrets when this was over.

"Lighten up, Robert, it's just sex. It's not like you're asking me to marry you or anything."

Maybe to her it was just sex, but not to him.

Get out of here. Stop this before you get hurt.

But how could he do that when his body burned so badly for her? He couldn't even think straight. He stared at her, awed by the sight of her lean coltish body. She was long of leg and narrow of waist, and the most beautiful woman he had ever seen. Her eyes flared at his frank appraisal, darkening to deep navy-blue, almost black.

The pulse of blood in his groin was hot, and when she reached up to cradle his face in her palms and kiss his lips lightly, sweetly, he groaned at the pleasure-pain of it.

She nibbled her way around his chin. He needed a shave and he heard his beard rasp against her skin, but she didn't seem to mind.

"Wait," he said. "We can't do this."

"We've already been over that, Robert. Just be in the moment, stop thinking and let yourself go."

"Can't," he gasped, so aroused he was barely able to speak. "No protection."

"Don't worry." She pulled open the drawer to her

bedside table and pulled out a three-pack of condoms. "Got us covered."

"Thank God," he croaked. "But I thought you haven't had sex in four years. Do you think the condoms are still good?"

"I have a confession," she whispered.

"Yeah?"

"I bought them the day after you came to work at Chez Remy."

"With me in mind?"

She grinned at him.

"Melanie."

"Robert," she breathed huskily.

That voice of hers got his blood pumping, and when she rubbed her breasts against him, he was sure he couldn't hold back much longer.

"It's been so long," he said. "I can't promise I'll be any good."

"That's why I'm going to take care of you first," she said. "And then when you get a second wind, it'll be my turn."

Slowly, trailing her hands down either side of his body, she sank to her knees.

"Melanie…" Robert groaned when he felt her warm breath against his throbbing skin.

She was a goddess.

He should tell her to get up, tell her not to do this, tell her that he wanted to be inside her, but he was just a man. And when the tip of her tongue flicked out to moisten the head of him, he was a goner one hundred percent.

She splayed her hands across his buttocks, and her mouth was sweet, velvet heat, her tongue an instrument of delicious torture.

She'd pushed him to the limits of his endurance. He tried to hold back, tried to resist, but he could not. She was just too damn wonderful.

His release was powerful, explosive. A ball of fire rolled along his nerve endings to lodge dead center in his aching shaft.

And then he left the earth, shot straight to the stars, and it was all her doing.

He collapsed backward onto the bed, pulling her with him. Panting, he closed his eyes, spent but still wanting more of her.

Laughing sneakily, she curled against his chest.

"Your turn now," he said, once he'd recovered somewhat. "And then we'll see who'll be snickering."

"What?"

He rolled her over onto her back, pinned her to the covers and stared down at her. She lay there looking up at him with those wide, trusting eyes, nibbling her bottom lip, nervous but excited.

Thoroughly, ravenously, he kissed her, and she kissed him back, and somewhere through his passion-addled brain came the realization that it had never been like this for him before.

Never.

TWENTY MINUTES LATER, Robert reached for her again.

"Come here, woman."

Melanie rolled into his arms, her bare belly pressed against his flat, rippled abdomen his hard erection pulsating against her thigh.

An erotic electricity shot through her entire body when his mouth claimed hers and his hand strayed to explore. His fingers made large circles at the triangle of hair below her navel, while his mouth teased hers.

Then his tongue went traveling south to the peaks of her jutting breasts. His tongue flicked out to lick one nipple, while his thumb rubbed the other, making her ache. His thigh tightened against her leg and his abdominal muscles hardened to pure, smooth steel.

"Robert…" She whispered his name with a sigh. She loved his name. Robert, Robert, Robert. "Robert, that feels so good."

Her eyes flew open and she lifted her head off the mattress. She had to see what he was doing to make her feel such exquisite pleasure and watched him draw her nipple into his mouth.

His tongue laved her sensitive skin as he suckled her deeply. She writhed against him, trying to push her body into his, needing more. Ribbons of sensation unfurled within her, and her inner muscles contracted with desire for him.

"Robert," she whispered weakly. "Robert."

"Yes, sweetheart. What do you want? Tell me what you need."

"I need you inside me. Now." She looked into his proud face, reached up to trace her finger along his scar, and felt something monumental move inside her. It was an emotion unlike anything she'd felt before. She couldn't name it.

She stopped trying to figure it out, just let it sweep her away.

He was kissing her again. Her mouth, her nose, her eyelids, her ears. He was over her and around her and then, at last, he was in her.

"Melanie…" He whispered her name, soft as an ocean breeze, caressing her with sound as he rotated his hips from side to side, maintaining tight, intense contact.

Now, with him deep in her moist heat, she felt every twitch of his muscles. He lit her up, a match to gasoline. She had no thoughts beyond wanting him deeper, thrust to the hilt.

She wrapped her legs around his waist and rocked him into her. Her fingers gripped his buttocks, drawing him closer. Her turn to own him. Her turn for control.

Frenzy.

She felt desperate, frantic need building inside her.

They came together and it was like pouring milk into milk. Infused with him, she could not tell where he began and she ended. No separation. Their connection was complete, and there was no space for anything else.

She bristled with joy. It rippled through her body, burning her to a crisp like a marshmallow in a campfire. She was warm and gooey and completely scorched, and she loved it.

When they separated and Melanie lay panting in his arms, the realization of what had just happened scared her witless.

HOURS LATER, Robert woke, squinted at the clock and saw it was four o'clock in the morning. The spot in the bed next to him was empty.

Melanie?

For one crazy moment, he thought she'd run out on him, and then he heard the sound of pots and pans clanging in the kitchen.

He rolled out of bed, put on her ex-husband's blue jeans and ran a hand through his hair to tame it before padding barefoot into the kitchen as he wrestled the T-shirt over his head. He found her standing at the counter, waffle ingredients lined up beside a big stainless steel bowl and an expensive looking but well-used Belgian waffle maker. Robert pulled the T-shirt down and tucked it into his waistband.

Their eyes met.

Pink splotches stained her cheeks. She was embarrassed at being caught staring at his chest. After last night? Her reaction surprised him and a rush of unexpected tenderness broadsided Robert.

"Your dream catcher's working overtime," she said. "I had a dream, about the ultimate waffle." Quickly she detailed the ingredients.

He was so immobilized by the sight of her that when something furry and hot brushed against his leg, he yelped, startled by the unexpected contact. Then he remembered the kitten.

Melanie grinned, glanced down and rubbed the cat's back with her big toe. "Stealth Kitty."

"You really should name her." Robert bent down to pick up the cat. "So you don't turn into Holly Golightly."

"But if I name her, I'll have to keep her."

"You're not planning on keeping her?"

"I'd like to but…"

"I dare you to name her."

Melanie rolled her eyes. "This isn't about the cat, is it?"

"What makes you say that?"

"You want to change me."

"I do not."

"Liar."

"You're so off base," he exclaimed, even though his heart crashed heavily against his chest. She was so damn right it hurt.

She studied him. "Your head isn't filling up with cutesy, happily-ever-after thoughts as we speak?"

"No," he declared.

"Okay, okay. I'll name the cat."

"What are you going to name her?"

"I don't know." Melanie glanced around the kitchen. "How about Waffle?"

"You certainly gave that a lot of consideration."

"It's a cat. She doesn't care what I call her just as long as I feed her. Here. Watch this." Melanie poured some milk in a bowl and set it on the floor. "Here Waffle, Waffle, Waffle."

The kitten darted over and began lapping up the milk.

Melanie glanced back at Robert and lifted her shoulders. "Waffle it is."

"Good thing you don't have kids," Robert said. "They'd have to go around with names like Banana and Cream of Wheat."

"Hey, what can I say?" Melanie giggled. "I love food. Besides, whenever I call her, it'll always remind me of our breakfast together."

She said it as if it was the only breakfast they would ever share. But he didn't want that to be true. When had he gotten to this point? He wondered.

"Speaking of food," he said glibly, rubbing his palms together. "Let's make some ultimate waffles."

Melanie fried bacon while Robert mixed up her recipe and then poured the batter into the steaming-hot waffle iron and closed the lid. Delicious smells filled the air.

When the waffles were done, he garnished them with whipped cream, powdered sugar and pecans. Melanie brought the bacon to the table along with maple syrup and two cups of hot coffee.

It turned out to be the best damn waffle Robert had ever put in his mouth.

Melanie took a bite and moaned with pleasure. "Now that's a waffle."

"It is pretty darn good."

"Not pretty darn good, Robert. It's the ultimate waffle."

Waffle meowed.

They laughed at the cat responding to her name, and Robert felt good inside in a way he hadn't in a very long time. The tip of Melanie's tongue flicked out to whisk away a dab of maple syrup at the corner of her mouth.

Robert's gaze drifted lazily down along her chin to the hollow of her throat and then to her chest. She wasn't wearing a bra beneath her thin T-shirt.

He couldn't help himself. He reached over and cupped her face in his hands. "Do you have any idea how beautiful you are?"

Her cheeks flushed. She was obviously embarrassed by his words.

His mouth took hers, and he tightened his fingers, on her warm skin. He wanted to touch her, hold her, love her.

The next thing he knew he had her in his arms and he was carrying her back to bed.

MELANIE LAY WITH HER FACE in the pillow, pretending to be asleep as Robert got up and padded into the bathroom. She heard the shower come on. Now that her passion had been extinguished, the reality of what they'd done crashed in on her like a house of Madam Lava's tarot cards.

Robert had told her he wasn't into casual sex, but she'd pushed him into it.

You didn't have to push very hard.

That was the scary thing. Did the fact that he'd been so easily persuaded mean he saw their relationship as much more than just sex? She thought about the way he'd looked at her in the throes of their lovemaking, and her throat tightened. There had been a lot of emotions in those sky-blue eyes.

What had she done?

They were such opposites. He was introverted, she was an extrovert. He liked to think things through, she preferred to plunge ahead. He wanted everything tied up in a neat tidy package, she was attracted to chaos.

If it's chaos you wanted, it's chaos you got.

She rolled over and stared at the ceiling. Robert was in the shower, humming. Yes, humming.

Things were worse than she'd thought.

The humming told her that he cared about her. A lot more than he should.

And they had to work together. He was her boss.

Chaos.

Damn it. How had she gotten herself into this?

Passion. That's what had done it. Passion would hamstring you every time.

Damn it, damn it, damn it.

What was she going to do now?

Quit. She would just quit and go back to Boston. Or call the headhunter at Chefs-to-Go and set up an interview with that restaurant in Seattle. Let Robert have the executive chef job at Chez Remy. He was much more suited for it, anyway.

But, selfishly, she didn't like the idea of not working around him anymore. She enjoyed their sparring and the way they'd learned to work together. It was fun, and now she'd gone and ruined it all by sleeping with him.

Just like she'd done with David.

What was the matter with her? Hadn't she learned anything from her past mistakes?

Uncertainty, that familiar enemy, seized hold of her.

"Rise and shine, wild thing." Robert came strolling from

the bathroom, toweling his hair dry. He had another towel wrapped around his lean waist and a big fat smile on his face. "We've got a big day ahead of us. The Charboneaux-Long rehearsal dinner is this evening."

God, he was acting all sweet and nice. Like a boyfriend. Like a husband. Melanie suppressed a shudder and forced herself to sit up.

Great. She felt like even more of a rat fink.

The sheet slipped and so did Robert's gaze, right down to her perky pink nipples peeping out from under the covers. Quickly, she snatched up the sheet and brought it to her neck.

"A little late for modesty. I've seen you naked and then some," he said.

It was a lot late, but better late than never, right?

"I've got to be honest," he said, and perched on the bed beside her.

"Uh-huh." She saw something in his eyes that made her heart lurch. Was that tenderness? Was he getting serious about her? He reached over and brushed a lock of hair from her forehead, and her stomach took a swoony little dive.

"You were quite something."

Damn that palm reader. Damn the rain that had stranded him overnight. Damn those sensational passionate waffles.

He looked so earnest, so happy. If only he weren't her boss. If only they weren't total opposites. If only she weren't scared to death of committing herself to something and failing yet again.

"But as much as I enjoyed it," he said, his smile fading, "I'm afraid you might have read more into this than there really is. I don't think it's such a good idea for us to do this again."

What?!

He was dumping her? Jilting her before they'd really even had a fling?

"I hope this won't affect our working relationship. I'm actually hoping that this got all the sexual tension out of our systems, and we can proceed as colleagues and friends."

He was letting her down easy. What had she done wrong? She thought what they'd just shared had been pretty darn good. Better than good. It had been exceptional. At least for her. He, on the other hand, must have been disappointed.

Robert stood up, towel still wrapped securely around his waist. "I just want you to know I have the utmost respect and admiration for you, Melanie."

Respect and admiration? She wanted to pummel him with her pillow. Respect and admiration? She wanted his undying love, not his frigging respect and admiration.

Love? Now that was a stupid thought. Since when did she want him falling in love with her?

He smiled and the look he gave her was exasperatingly platonic. To hell with hitting him with a pillow. She wanted to double up her fist and punch him in his sexy, straight white teeth.

"Pstt." She waved a hand. "We had a good time. Sex is just sex. Doesn't have to mean anything more than that, right?"

"I'm glad you understand."

"Sure, sure. No biggie. In fact, I'm relieved you aren't making this out to be some huge thing."

So she was nothing but a booty call? That was it? She couldn't figure out why that upset her. Two minutes ago, she'd been agonizing over how to break the news to him that he couldn't think long term where she was concerned, and now he was saying exactly that to her.

Apparently she'd been quite mistaken. He didn't harbor any deep feelings for her at all.

The beast.

"So we're cool." He looked relieved.

"Like ice, baby," she lied. "Like ice."

But if that was true, why did she suddenly feel as if her heart had melted into a puddle of tears?

CHAPTER THIRTEEN

"I'VE GOT TO TALK TO YOU." Breathlessly, Melanie grabbed Sylvie's elbow and dragged her off into the corner of the art gallery.

If Chez Remy reflected their father's Cajun heritage, the upscale art galley mirrored their mother's Creole background. When Melanie was a child, an outside operator had rented the gallery from Anne and sold art pertaining mostly to the French Quarter. But now, under Sylvie's influence, the flavor of the gallery had changed. Sylvie had been in touch with local artists and was featuring more contemporary painters and sculptors from across Louisiana. She'd also introduced jewelry created by a New Orleans artists' co-op, and it had proven a big success.

The gallery took up two floors of the hotel and had both a street and hotel entrance. It was a long and narrow space with stairs leading up to a mezzanine and loft that gave the place a spacious, airy feel.

"I need help," Melanie whispered, casting a quick glance over her shoulder to make sure Sylvie's assistant—who was in the process of setting up an exhibit featuring an up-and-coming local sculptor who made beautiful art from the debris left in the aftermath of Hurricane Katrina—wasn't listening.

"You? You're asking for advice?"

"Yes, me. I know I haven't taken advice well in the past, but I'm desperate, Syl. I feel so strung out."

"Strung out?" A troubled expression crossed her sister's face. "What do you mean, strung out?"

"Too much rum last night." *And too much Robert.*

"That's right, the bachelorette auction was last night. How'd it go? Besides too much rum?"

"It was amazing."

"The bachelorette auction was amazing?"

"No, no." Melanie shook her head. "Not that. What happened after."

"What did happen after?"

"The Phantom of the Opera and I went on a carousel ride, and it was so much fun and it started to rain and…"

"You're not making any sense. Are you all right?"

"No. No, I'm not." Melanie placed a hand to her forehead and paced the gallery. "I've never felt like this. I'm scared. I'm freaked. I'm in trouble."

Sylvie looked concerned. "First, you have to calm down. Right now, you're scaring me," she said.

Melanie knew that she was babbling. She wanted to tell her sister about Robert. About how they'd made love last night and it had been incredible. How they'd made breakfast together and it had been freakin' awesome, until, for no reason at all Robert had gotten weird on her and run away. But she was so full of these jumbled, crazy feelings she didn't know how to say what she wanted to say. It was coming out all mixed up.

She thought about the way Robert's mouth fitted over hers, the way his body made her feel—like she was worth a million dollars. She thought about how much fun she had being with him, but he considered her nothing more than a casual fling. Then again, that was how she'd billed herself to him. What had she expected?

Still, she hadn't expected it to hurt as much as it did. Somewhere along the way she'd started thinking about him as much more than a casual fling. She tried to pinpoint when it had actually occurred, but there didn't seem to be one particular moment. It had just crept up on her gradually, until he dominated her every waking thought.

"Auntie Mel, Auntie Mel!" Sylvie's daughter, Daisy Rose, red curls flying, ran to fling herself into Melanie's arms.

Melanie caught her niece and swung her high in the air, her childish squeals of delight echoing off the walls. She wore an adorable pink dress with ruffles, and matching pink ballet slippers with white tights.

"Where did you come from?"

"I was in my playhouse." She pointed to the adjoining cloakroom that Sylvie had converted into a playroom for Daisy Rose.

"How's my favorite girl this morning?" Melanie asked, and chucked her playfully under the chin.

"One hundred percent," she said in the cutest little singsong voice.

"One hundred percent?" Melanie looked at Sylvie.

"She picked that phrase up from Jefferson," Sylvie explained, referring to her fiancé.

Melanie looked back at Daisy Rose. "Not fifty percent?"

The child shook her head.

"Not eighty-eight point six percent?"

"Nope." Exuberantly, Daisy Rose shot her chubby little arms into the air and squirmed against Melanie. "One hundred percent."

"She's really wound up this morning, aren't you, precious?" Sylvie leaned over to kiss the top of her daughter's head. "I'm having a dilly of a time trying to get any work done."

"No babysitter this morning?"

"Mom's taking her to be photographed." Sylvie laughed. "As if we don't have enough pictures."

"But I'm pretty," Daisy Rose said unabashedly.

"And stunningly modest." Sylvie added with a grin.

How great it was that little Daisy Rose was growing up at the hotel, just as Melanie and her sisters had. Although as a child she hadn't realized it, the Hotel Marchand was a very special place.

Melanie remembered how the gallery looked through preschooler eyes. A room that echoed nicely when she used to run up and down on the hardwood floors in her tap shoes and make all the adults frown. She thought of how she used to lie on the floor, and look up at the paintings and pretend she was in them—walking along country roads, boating down bayous, climbing the stairways of lush plantation homes.

Growing up here had spoiled her for the ordinary. Maybe that was one of the reasons she was always on the lookout for the next new adventure, the next new recipe to try, the next good-looking guy to flirt with. She was trying to recapture her exotic childhood.

Funny, everything she'd ever wanted was right here where she'd started.

"Sylvie?" The sound of their mother's honey-coated voice and the click of her shoes echoed smartly against the hardwood floors.

"Back here, Mother," Sylvie called out.

"I gotta go." Melanie didn't want her mom to see her like this, incoherent over a man. She knew Anne would remember how besotted she'd been over David.

"Wait, wait." Sylvie put a restraining hand on her arm. "I thought you needed my advice."

"It's okay. I'm all right. I can deal with this on my own." She slipped out the back exit, heart pounding, enveloped by the same panicky sensation that had caused her to leave home when she was eighteen. The same sensations that had kept her from coming back to New Orleans to live when everything and everyone she loved was right here. It weighed her down, heavy as claustrophobia.

Melanie was afraid of caring too deeply, of depending too much on those she loved. Because, rational or not, a part of her believed that total emotional commitment would stifle her passion, her creative drive. And without her passion for life, her creativity in the kitchen, who would she be?

Panic driven, she plucked the cell phone from her waistband, found a quiet alcove and made a call to the headhunter at Chefs-to-Go. Five minutes later, she'd scheduled a job interview in Seattle.

CHARLOTTE WAS TRYING HER best to remain cool, calm and collected on a day that promised to be insanely busy.

She glanced up to see Luc Carter striding across the lobby toward her, a look of concern on his face.

"Charlotte, could I have a word?"

"Let's go into my office." She led the way as an ominous feeling swept over her.

"We've got a big problem." Luc plowed a hand through his hair once they were in her office with the door closed.

"What now?"

"There's been a major snafu over the block of rooms reserved for the Charboneaux-Long wedding."

"What do you mean by 'snafu'?"

"The rooms have been double booked."

"Oh, this is terrible." Charlotte sat down at her desk and motioned for Luc to take a seat, but he remained standing. "How did this happen? The wedding has been planned for over a year."

"I don't know," Luc said. "I'm trying my best to get to the bottom of it."

"What have you done so far?"

"I'm working with reservations, but some of the guests are already here. We've put the wedding party in their assigned rooms and relocated the other guests to surrounding hotels. We'll have to offer comps and we'll need extra help shuttling the guests to their new locations."

Thank heaven for Luc. He was a godsend.

"Good work," she said. "I'll start rounding up what employees I can find for shuttle duty."

"I'm on it," Luc said, and hurried from her office.

Charlotte dropped her head into her hands. What had happened with the Charboneaux-Long reservations? Was it an intentional screwup, or had it just been an oversight? It was becoming increasingly difficult to believe the latter.

Who would want to destroy the Hotel Marchand? It was a question Charlotte had been asking herself for the last few weeks.

You're a Marchand, she reminded herself. *You can handle this, and the family is counting on you.*

Resolutely, Charlotte took in a shaky breath and ran a

hand over her hair to smooth it. The day was extra humid and her hair was starting to frizz. She'd have to pop up to her mother's room and straighten it, because today was an important day. If she couldn't control anything else, at least she could control her hair.

She stood and headed for the hallway, but she hadn't taken two steps from her office when Sylvie came running toward her. "Charlotte," she said breathlessly, "I think maybe you were right."

"About what?"

"Melanie. She told me she was strung out. Oh God, Charlotte. Our baby sister's using drugs!"

THE ATMOSPHERE IN THE kitchen was strained. Everyone was tense over the extra pressure caused by the mix-up in the wedding party's hotel reservations. Nothing—absolutely nothing—could go wrong with tonight's dinner.

But Robert couldn't seem to make himself care. The only thing that concerned him was making sure that he'd fooled Melanie about his true feelings for her.

His gut was twisted in knots and he felt an almost overwhelming urge to punch something. Good thing he was so adept at hiding his emotions. Otherwise, Melanie would have seen right through that bull he'd spouted back there at her apartment.

He barked orders to the prep cooks and yelled at the waiters who had come in early to help set up the private dining room. Plus, Charlotte was hovering in the kitchen, micromanaging the event and making him even jumpier.

Damn. He shouldn't have had that third cup of coffee. But he'd needed something to take his mind off what had happened with Melanie. Unfortunately, overdosing on caffeine had the opposite effect of what he'd been shooting for. It both narrowed and highly tuned his focus, and all he could remember was what had gone on in the wee hours of the morning in Melanie's bed.

Melanie appeared to be doing her best to avoid him, too. Whenever he came into the kitchen, she would disappear into the private dining room to fuss with something inconsequential like the napkin placements. Whenever business drove him into the dining room, she would pop back into the melee in the kitchen, head down, rarely glancing his way, as if she was embarrassed.

One way or the other, they would get through this. Time would pass and eventually everything would be all right again. He was pretty sure she'd bought his story. That she had no clue as to how he really felt.

So why did you tell her that sex was all it was?

To save face. To salvage his pride. To save her the trouble of dumping him later on.

Work. Just concentrate on your work.

But he'd been doing that for so long, and while it kept his mind busy, it never really seemed to fix the deep abiding loneliness he felt.

"How's everything coming along?" Charlotte asked, peering over Robert's shoulder, double-checking the food preparations.

"Perfect," he said tersely.

"Seems a little chaotic in here," she observed.

"Don't worry. Kitchen on a deadline. Nothing out of the ordinary."

"Could I speak to you privately?" Charlotte asked.

"What?" Robert was barely listening. He had an eye on Melanie, who'd just come through the door with an armful of fresh crawfish and was heading for the prep sink.

Charlotte nodded in the direction of his office. "Could we step out of the line of fire for a brief chat?"

"Right now?"

"Please."

"Yeah, sure." He wiped his hands on his apron and turned to follow her into his office. He noticed that Melanie was watching him from the corner of her eye.

Charlotte shut the door behind them. "I'm very worried about Melanie," she said.

"Uh-huh?"

"She's hasn't seemed like herself lately, and this morning she told Sylvie she was strung out. Do you think she could be doing drugs?"

"Melanie's not doing drugs." Robert had to work hard to keep the irritation out of his voice. "It's a tense day, Charlotte."

"I know that." She took a deep breath. "But I'm afraid she'll make a mistake with the rehearsal dinner."

"She's fine. She's not going to make a mistake."

Charlotte reached out to touch his forearm. "You seem pretty tense, too, Robert. Is there something you need to tell me?"

Hell, yeah, I think I'm falling in love with your sister and she does not love me back.

"Rest assured, Charlotte, everything is going to be all right. Melanie will settle down. Now I really do have to get back to work if you want this meal to come off."

"Yes, yes, of course. I'll let you do your job and I'll go do mine," Charlotte said, excusing herself.

"We got problems, boss," Jean-Paul stated as Robert stepped back into the kitchen. "That ground turkey you ordered for the canapés isn't here."

"What do you mean, it's not here?"

Jean-Paul shrugged. "Never showed up from the supplier."

"Did you call them?"

"Yep. They said they delivered it last night, but we have no record of it."

Robert swore under his breath. He glanced at his watch, saw how tight they were for time and swore again. He'd have to send someone to the grocery store to pick up what they needed. He looked around the room and realized he had little staff to spare. Everyone was working at top speed, doing several tasks at once. Even as they were talking, Jean-Paul was busy shucking the husks off fresh corn.

"Excuse me," Melanie said, squeezing past him and Jean-Paul. Her elbow accidentally brushed against his hip and Robert's heart tumbled all the way to his shoes.

To heck with it; he'd go after the ground turkey himself. If he could just get away from Melanie for a little while he could collect himself, get a handle on his emotions and survive this day.

"Continue with the rest of the preparations," Robert told Jean-Paul. "I'll go after the turkey."

"WHERE'S ROBERT GOING?" Melanie asked Jean-Paul.

"The ground turkey for the canapés never showed up. He went to get some."

What else would go wrong? Melanie wondered. She glanced at the clock. "We're working down to the wire. Do we have anything in the refrigerator we could substitute for turkey?"

"We've got plenty of fresh crabmeat."

"Great, let's substitute that."

If Robert had just talked to her about the problem with the menu, she could have saved him a trip to the store.

"Listen up, people." She clapped her hands. "There's been a change in plans. We're substituting crabmeat for turkey in the canapés. Now hop to it. Time is of the essence."

THE SKY WAS OVERCAST and twilight was beginning to fall as Robert walked to the parking lot a short distance from the hotel. He headed to the farthest corner from the street, where he'd parked his car.

He heard footsteps behind him, but thought nothing of it until a man's voice he didn't recognize called out, "Hey, buddy."

Robert turned to see who it was and felt a blow to the back of his head.

The last thing he remembered before he lost consciousness was two shady-looking men dragging him across the cement.

WHERE WAS ROBERT? Melanie fretted. He'd been gone over an hour. Good thing she hadn't waited for him to start making the canapés.

She tried him on his cell phone but he didn't answer. She left a message on his voice mail, telling him to call her as soon as he got the message.

Worry gnawed at her. What if he'd been in an accident? It wasn't like responsible Robert not to answer his phone or to take so long over a simple errand. Then again, she hadn't thought he was the kind of guy who'd have sex with her and then just dump her, either.

Face it, Mel, you don't know him. Not really.

What if the stress had gotten to him and he'd gone off to search for cocaine?

That thought sent a cold chill through her.

She briefly considered telling Charlotte that Robert was MIA, but immediately decided against it. Her sister was stressed to the max. She didn't need this on top of everything else.

Resolutely, Melanie decided Robert must have gotten caught in traffic and forgotten to recharge the batteries in his cell phone. No point freaking out until there was something to freak out about.

FIVE MINUTES AFTER the appetizers had been served to the members of the Charboneaux-Long wedding party, Leo the bartender came barreling from the dining room into the kitchen looking as if he'd just encountered Frankenstein's monster.

"Duck and cover, Mel," Leo panted. "Here comes Bridezilla."

"Who?" Melanie looked up from the salad she was assembling for the second course.

"Carly Charboneaux, the bride-to-be!" The high-pitched screech came from the deranged-looking young woman marching into the kitchen behind the bartender. "And I demand to know who's responsible for this…this…fiasco." In her hand she held a squashed crabmeat canapé up in a paper napkin.

"Is something wrong with the food?" Melanie wiped her hands on her apron.

"Is something wrong with the food?" she shrieked. "My maid of honor is highly allergic to crabmeat. I told your executive chef that months ago and he assured me I had nothing to worry about. Now Amy's face is swelling up like a balloon."

"What?" Fear squeezed Melanie's heart as she shot past Carly toward into the private room where the dinner was being held.

She found a young woman sitting at one of the tables, surrounded by a cluster of people. Melanie raced over and saw that the poor woman's face was pink and puffy.

"I'll be okay," Amy said. "I just needed a shot of Benadryl. I carry it in my purse."

"You should go to a doctor," Melanie said.

"My fiancé is a doctor." The maid of honor placed a hand on the shoulder of the man sitting beside her.

That made Melanie feel slightly better.

"Really," he said. "Amy will be all right. Carly is making a bigger deal of this than she needs to."

"Amy looks like a freak and my wedding is tomorrow. It's a disaster. Everything is ruined."

"The swelling will be all gone by then," Amy's fiancé assured Carly. "I promise."

"Miss Charboneaux, Amy," Melanie said, "I am deeply, deeply sorry for the mistake. I'm completely responsible. I made the last minute substitutions to the menu without the executive chef's knowledge. Let me make this right."

"Just you wait. When I get through suing this hotel, you won't have a pot to…" Carly shook her finger under Melanie's nose.

"Carly, honey, you've got to calm down," The mother of the bride said as she trailed behind her daughter.

"Calm down? Calm down? How do you expect me to calm down? First they screw up our allotment of rooms and now they've put crab in the canapés and made Amy swell up."

"Carly, look at me," Amy said. "The swelling is already going down. It's okay."

A vein in the bride-to-be's forehead was so prominent Melanie feared the girl would keel over. She could just imagine the lawsuit if Carly fainted and cracked her head open on the floor.

Carly burst into tears. "It's an omen. A terrible omen. The marriage is going to be a disaster. Call off the wedding, Mother. Send everyone home. My marriage is doomed."

"We'll refund your money for the rehearsal dinner," Melanie said. "And we'll compensate Amy for any medical expenses incurred due to eating the crabmeat." It wasn't her place to offer the Charboneaux a refund or to take on Amy's medical expenses, but she'd pay for it out of her own pocket if she had to.

"Please, everyone," Amy said. "Let's not make a fuss. Accidents happen."

"Where's your general manager?" Mrs. Charboneaux said. "I want to speak to her. Right now."

This was the last thing Charlotte needed, Melanie decided.

"I will make this up to you," she promised. "I'll prepare a special dessert and it'll be complimentary like the entire meal. Please, please forgive my mistake. We'll bring in the second course. Go back to your celebration."

After making sure that Amy really was okay, Melanie returned to the kitchen.

"Okay, people, we've got to get the second course out there, right now."

She drew aside the busboy. "Raoul, I'm going to give you a grocery list. Go get these items for me now and get back here as quickly as possible."

The young man nodded. She made out a list sent him on his way, and then she went to help serve up the second course. With any luck, she could salvage her reputation and keep Charlotte from finding out about her mistake in the process.

CHAPTER FOURTEEN

MELANIE WAS PLANNING an extravagant gesture to redeem herself. She had to show the Charboneaux and their guests how extremely sorry she was for her mistake.

Raoul had returned with the ingredients she needed and she was assembling the cherries jubilee when Jean-Paul ambled over.

"You're going to do a flambé?" He arched an eyebrow.

"It's going to be the grand finale to the meal—which, by the way, crabmeat canapé fiasco aside, everyone is raving about." She spoke in a rush.

"You ever done a flambé, *chère?*"

"Sure, lots of times." At home, not for guests, but come on, how hard could it be?

"Why don't you get Allison to do it?"

"Because for one, Allison is working on the wedding cake for tomorrow, and two, I'm the one the Charboneaux are mad at. I have to save face. I can't let them leave with a bad taste in their mouth for Chez Remy and the Hotel Marchand."

"But are you trained in proper flambé technique?"

"What is this? Twenty questions? Are you going to help me or not?"

Jean-Paul shrugged. "Okay, but all the responsibility is on you."

"Of course." She waved a hand. "Let's get these cherries loaded up on the cart."

The wedding party was in the process of making celebratory toasts when Melanie pushed the flambé cart to one side of the table, parking it near the big picture window that looked out on the French Quarter. While they finished their toasts, she turned on the portable gas burners and announced her surprise, which was met with enthusiastic applause.

"I've never had cherries jubilee," Carly said. "This should be fun."

Melanie put the cherries into the saucepans until they were thoroughly heated, and when they were ready, she added the cherry brandy.

Striking a long kitchen match, she lit the liqueur fumes.

The cherries flambéed.

The guests gasped with delight as the flames licked up.

The applause and smiling faces were like a soothing balm to her conscience. There, she'd done everything she could to right her mistake, and she felt much better

But the flames were already burning out. Maybe if she put just a tipple more brandy in, she could prolong the show.

She reached for the bottle of brandy and liberally laced the cherries with more liquor.

Whoosh!

The flames leaped from the pan, following the arc of alcohol.

"My God," Carly Charboneaux cried. "The place is on fire."

"Don't panic," Melanie said as she grabbed the flambé pan's oversize lid and dropped it over the flaming cherries. "I've got everything under control. Fire's all out, see?"

But no one was listening to her. Chairs were being knocked

over and people were screaming as they stampeded for the door.

And that's when she saw the flames had ignited the curtains.

Not only that, but her apron as well.

She was on fire.

Redemption, she decided in that moment, had come at a steep price.

ROBERT CAME TO IN THE parking lot, slumped over the hood of his car. His head was throbbing and his back ached.

What the hell?

It took him a moment to remember what had happened. His hand immediately went to his wallet. It was gone.

He'd been mugged.

Groaning, Robert stumbled to his feet. His head swam dizzily. He stood there a moment, taking in deep breaths, trying to get his bearings and orient himself.

What time was it? He squinted at his watch.

Good God, it was seven-thirty.

He'd been out over two hours and the rehearsal dinner was in progress. So much for the canapés. The Charboneaux were going to be thoroughly pissed off.

He had to get back to the restaurant and smooth things over. Head reeling, he staggered back to the hotel and entered the private dining room, intent on apologizing profusely to the wedding party for not delivering on the canapés.

Chaos greeted him.

People were screaming and running for the exits.

And then he saw the source of the panic.

Fire!

Fear shot a bolus of adrenaline through Robert's veins. He

walked into the dining room just in time to see Melanie's apron catch flame.

Melanie was on fire!

Beware of fire, Madam Lava had told him.

Damn, it seemed as if the crone had been right...

Robert was galvanized into action while everyone else trampled over one another to get out of the room. His head cleared instantly and he dashed to the fire extinguisher mounted on the wall. It took him only a few seconds to get there, but it felt as if he were moving in slow motion through the Louisiana swamp.

Melanie's eyes were wide as she batted at the flames licking up her apron. A deep sense of calm settled over Robert, allowing him to function rationally. He detached himself from his emotions. Felt nothing as he grabbed the extinguisher and pulled the pin. Aiming the nozzle, he depressed the trigger, showering Melanie in white CO_2 foam, instantly dousing the fire. When her burning apron was extinguished, he turned to the curtains and blitzed those flames into oblivion, too.

It was a surreal experience. Robert couldn't have been calmer if he'd popped a twenty milligram Valium. Melanie just stood there, clearly in shock.

He took off her scorched apron and tossed it to the floor. He examined her body, looking for damage. She shivered, her teeth chattering.

Thankfully, he found no burns. He had gotten to her in time.

"Are you hurt?" he asked quietly.

She shook her head. "I don't know. I don't think so but I can't really feel anything. I'm numb."

Me, too.

Robert looked up to see that Luc was in the room, trying to calm the guests who had not gotten out. Robert had no doubt Charlotte would be showing up as soon as she heard what had happened.

He wanted first crack at Melanie before her sister got to her. Gently, he took her by the shoulders and led her into the kitchen.

"Out," he told the cooks and the wait staff. "Everyone get out. Go clean up the private dining room."

His employees stared at him.

"But, boss," Jean-Paul said, "we're in the middle of dinner rush."

"Turn your fires off. Get out of the kitchen. Ten minutes." He pointed to the door.

His staff stopped what they were doing, turned off the gas burners and filed solemnly out of the room.

Once everyone had cleared out, Robert lost it.

He spun on his heel to face Melanie. "What in God's name were you thinking, woman? No, wait." Angrily, he snapped his fingers twice. "I've got it. You weren't thinking. Just Melanie doing whatever pops into her head without a single thought for the consequences. Not caring one damn bit who she hurts in the process."

"I care," Melanie mumbled.

He saw the tears glistening in her eyes, saw her hands trembling and knew that she was scared and shaken. But, damn it, he was scared, too. She could have been badly hurt. He could have lost her tonight.

The stark truth of it was almost more than he could bear.

Robert clenched his teeth. He felt stripped naked, raw, vulnerable. Anger and fear and love wadded in his throat and he could not swallow.

"Robert," she whispered. "I'm so sorry."

"So am I." He couldn't look at her. If he looked at her face, saw the insecurity in her indigo eyes, he knew he would break down. He found a spot just above her head and stared at a crack in the wall, cramming his feelings down tight inside him.

But the emotions refused to go away. He'd finally called up his long-buried feelings and now they would not leave. For better or worse, he was stuck with them.

"What do you think you were doing with that flambé fiasco!" He rubbed a hand over his mouth. "That wasn't part of the dinner. What you did was inexcusable."

"I know," she wailed.

"Guests could have been hurt. Damn it, Melanie you could have been…" He could not finish the sentence. He thought of her scar, what she had already suffered, and his gut twisted.

She sank her hands on her hips. "Who are you to criticize me, Robert LeSoeur? I might be foolish at times, and impulsive and too high-spirited, but at least I'm not a liar and I own up to my mistakes. I take responsibility for what I've done. What happened in the dining room is entirely my fault and I'll do whatever it takes to make amends. I won't blame it on someone else or get someone to do damage control for me. I'm going to face the Charboneaux. I'm going to make this right."

"What do you mean, you're not a liar? What did I lie about?"

"You know."

"No," he said, perplexed by her outburst. "No, I don't."

"Fourteen years ago you were arrested for possession of cocaine, but lucky you. You had a high-powered district attorney aunt who got you off scot-free. Ring any bells, Robert?"

He stared at her, disturbed both by what she'd said and what he was feeling. "How do you know about all that?"

"So you're not going to deny it like you did last night at my place? When you lied straight to my face and told me you'd never been arrested, that you've never done drugs?"

"I've never done drugs. Ever."

"But you have been arrested."

He said nothing.

"Oh yeah." The CO_2 foam was starting to dissipate, but she still looked as if she could pass for the hotel poltergeist. "I'm sure you were just wrongly accused. Someone must have planted the cocaine on you. Framed you."

Robert's breath rattled in his lungs. He thought he'd put this far behind him, thought he'd buried it away for good. Well, except for the darkness that overtook him from time to time. How long did a man have to pay the price for a mistake?

"Where did you get this information?" he demanded.

"I have my sources."

He knew then that she was the one who'd had someone call the Stratosphere to ask about him. It had been her, not Charlotte, as he'd supposed.

"You had me investigated." He didn't know which hurt more, the fact that she'd had done so or that she was so ready to believe the accusations against him.

"I had to find out about the man my mother had given complete control of my father's kitchen."

"You were going to use the information to get rid of me," he said flatly. He couldn't wrap his head around what she'd done, and it hurt more than he wanted to admit.

She didn't deny it.

"You can think whatever you like, Melanie, but the drugs weren't mine. I took the rap for a friend."

"A likely story."

"Believe it or not, it's the truth." He shrugged. "At this point I don't really care anymore."

"Who was this friend and why did you take the rap for him?"

"That's all I'm going to say on the subject."

"Why? If it's true, why not tell me all the details?"

"Because," he said, "I don't trust you."

She flinched.

He saw that he'd struck to the heart of her insecurities. Her trustworthiness was a touchy issue. She wanted people to trust in her, but she shied from the responsibility that came with it. Robert hadn't meant to hurt her feelings, but she needed to hear the truth.

"I was beginning to think that maybe we could have more than just sex," she said. "That we could have a future together—you know, work out our differences. That we were actually good together *because* of our differences. That we balanced each other out. But now I know that was a foolish dream. I can't be with a man who doesn't trust me."

"And I can't be with a woman who sets spies on me," he said to the woman he loved, the woman who had just stabbed him in the back.

THE JOYOUS SOUNDS of free-flowing jazz, the blatantly outrageous costumes, the growing crowds on Bourbon Street announced that Mardi Gras celebrations were heating up. The French Quarter hadn't been this lively since before Katrina, but Melanie felt utterly miserable as she trudged through the streets.

She could still see the anger in Robert's eyes when he'd realized she'd had him investigated.

He'd said he'd taken the drug rap for someone else. She wanted so badly to believe him.

Misery ate at her. Robert thought she was capable of using the information she'd uncovered to get her own way. And how could she blame him? She had given him no reason to trust her.

She'd lost him and there was nothing to do but leave town. She didn't fit in here, anyway. Even when she tried to do the right thing it seemed to blow up in her face. Her family got along just fine without her. She'd go to that job interview in Seattle, and if they offered her the job, she was taking it.

CHARLOTTE WAS SITTING in her office, exhausted, drained from the day's events, but she could not make herself go home. She couldn't stop thinking about Melanie and how seriously she could have been hurt.

Both Robert and Luc had stepped up to the plate, calming the guests, dealing with the fire department, handling the rest of the mess while Charlotte smoothed things over with the Charboneaux. With the help of her staff, she'd managed to weather that particular storm, but there was another one brewing—confronting Melanie about her drug use. The time had come. Charlotte was going to have to get their mother involved.

The ringing of the phone startled her. It was almost eleven. A call this late usually spelled trouble. Bracing herself for a fresh onslaught of problems, she picked it up. "Hello?"

"Char, it's Melanie."

"Mellie, thank goodness. Are you okay? Robert said you two had a fight."

"I'm fine."

"Are you sure?"

"Listen, Charlotte. I'm going to take off for a few days. I need some time alone."

"Sweetie, no. Don't go anywhere. Come to the hotel where we can talk. Or better yet, I'll come over to your place. We can help you through this."

"I'm not at home."

"Where are you?"

"At the airport. I'm about to board a plane to Seattle."

"You're going up there to interview for a job."

"Yes."

"Running away isn't going to solve your problem," Charlotte said.

"I can't stay where I don't fit in."

"What are you talking about? Of course you fit in."

"It's the final boarding call. I'll be back on Monday night."

"Come to the hotel as soon as you get in. We have to talk about this."

"Tell Robert…"

"Tell Robert what?"

"I gotta go."

Concern knotted Charlotte's chest. "Melanie…" she said, but she was talking to a dial tone.

"Ms. MARCHAND?" Robert tapped on the open door to Charlotte's office and he was surprised to find Anne sitting behind the desk, leafing through a photo album.

The woman looked up and broke into a welcoming smile. "Robert, come in, come in."

"I was looking for Charlotte."

"She went up to my quarters to get something for me." Robert knew that Anne had recently moved back to the hotel. She'd been staying at her mother's house since her recent heart attack. "May I help you?" she asked.

He moved into the room, feeling the old familiar sadness dragging down his heart.

"Is something wrong?" Anne asked, sliding off her reading glasses.

"I need to give you this." He passed her an envelope.

She opened it up, scanned the letter and then looked up at him, concern in her eyes. "I don't understand. You're leaving us?"

"Yes, ma'am."

"I know you're a very private person, Robert, but do you mind my asking why? Haven't we treated you well here?"

He shifted his weight. This was much more difficult than he'd thought it was going to be. He loved the Hotel Marchand. It was the best place he'd ever worked. He loved the people, especially the Marchand family, and already felt a fierce loyalty toward them. But he had to go.

Maybe that was the problem. He was never meant to be happy. He'd been born into sadness and loneliness and that was where he was meant to stay.

"Everyone has been wonderful. I'm leaving for personal reasons."

"Do those reasons have anything to do with my youngest daughter?"

He nodded.

"Robert, I'm going to ask you something and I want you to be perfectly honest with me."

"Yes, Mrs. Marchand."

"Do you think Melanie is using drugs?"

He met the older woman's eyes and saw in her gaze both steely determination and exquisite tenderness. She could dish out tough love or tender loving care, whatever was required of her. She was a strong woman, a survivor, and he saw her admirable character traits in Melanie. "No, I do not."

Anne let out her breath in a soft, ladylike sigh. "All right then, I have only one more question."

"Still want me to be perfectly honest?"

"Always, Robert. I highly value honesty."

"What's your question?"

"Are you in love with Melanie?"

He met her eyes and didn't flinch. "With a passion that scares me more than anything ever has, Mrs. Marchand. And that's the very reason I have to resign."

CHAPTER FIFTEEN

"I KNOW IT'S LATE but I need a place to crash." Melanie stood on Coby's doorsteps, the tears she'd cried on the long flight now dried.

Her friend threw his door open wide. "For you, toots, anything."

She stepped over the threshold and shrugged off her backpack, letting it slide to the floor, then followed Coby into his living room.

"Take a load off. You look like you could use a drink. What'll you have?"

"Whatever."

"I'm all out of whatever. How about a rum and Coke?"

She'd had a rum and Coke last night with Robert. At the memory, fresh tears pressed against her eyelids. Had it only been last night that they'd made love? So much had happened, it felt like a decade ago. "I'd rather have wine."

"Red or white?" Coby called from the kitchen.

"Red."

"So what's his name?" he asked, as he sashayed back into the room with two glasses of wine in his hands.

"How do you know this is about a man?"

"Please, toots." Coby sat beside her on the couch and

crossed his legs. "I know man trouble when I see it. Go ahead, I'm listening."

"It's Robert LeSoeur."

"Somehow I knew you were going to say that."

Melanie sighed. "But it's more than just man trouble."

"Uh-huh."

"It's my family. No matter how hard I try to fit in, I just don't. A headhunter called me about a position as executive chef at La Chère and I'm here for an interview."

"Get out! I'm interviewing for that job, too."

"Oh no, Coby, really?"

"It wouldn't be the first time we were up for the same job."

"You're not jealous?"

"Toots, you can cook circles around me, but let's face facts, bossing people about isn't your forte. I, on the other hand—" he made a cracking noise and mimicked cracking a whip "—love it."

"You're saying you're going to score the job over me?" she challenged.

"I'm saying you're in love with Robert LeSoeur, and as soon as you admit that to yourself, you'll be heading back to New Orleans."

"Who says I'm in love with him?"

"You don't have to say it, toots. You flew all the way up here to get away from him. The man has got to be under your skin."

"But how can I be in love with a man who can't talk to me? I confronted him about his cocaine conviction and he didn't deny it, but claims he took the rap for a friend. That's all he'd tell me. He says he can't trust me because I had you investigate him."

"It's not very trustworthy behavior," Coby pointed out.

"Yes, but that was before I really knew him. Coby, there's something about him. He's suffered so much but he won't talk about it. He's kept himself so shut down emotionally that I think he's looking for any excuse not to open up to me." She blinked to keep from crying again.

"If he can't share himself with you, then I don't see that you've got a future together."

"Me, either."

"If only there was some way you could find out the truth," Coby said. "What if you went to see his aunt?"

"Congresswoman Longren?"

"That'd be the one."

"But I'm sure I can't just walk in off the street and get a meeting with her."

Coby winked. "You're in luck, toots. I just happen to know where Pamela Longren has brunch every Sunday."

ROBERT LAY IN HIS BED, unable to sleep.

Anne Marchand had refused to accept his resignation. "I never figured you for the type of man who ran out on a friend in need."

Guilt claimed him then. The only thing that could have been more persuasive was what came out of her mouth next.

"Robert, we consider you part of the family. You belong here. Please, don't go. We need you. Melanie needs you."

"Melanie doesn't need anyone," he'd replied with a shake of his head. "She's the most independent woman I've ever met."

Anne smiled. "That's what she wants you to think. That girl wants to settle down so badly she can taste it. She just doesn't know how to go about it, and after that mistake she made with David, she's scared to try again. Don't let her push you away, Robert. You're good for each other. You temper her impetuousness and she's brought you out of your shell. And yes, I've noticed."

He'd nodded. What Anne had said was true.

"So please, if you really love her, take this back." She'd extended his resignation. "Stay here. Fight for her."

"I just don't see how it can work between us. Our temperaments are polar opposites."

"But don't you understand? That's what makes you so good together. You balance each other out. Like my Rémy and me. Melanie's father was just like her—passionate, creative, impulsive, daring. Believe me, Robert, you're in for the ride of your life."

The ride of his life.

Did he really want that?

He'd spent his life trying to be calm and sedate and controlled. But with Melanie he felt decidedly out of control. He felt wild and adventuresome and alive, truly alive for the first time in his life.

If he left now, he would never realize his full potential.

And in his heart, he knew he would never find anyone else he loved as much.

Why didn't you tell her all this after you made love? Why did you pretend it was just about sex?

He'd done it to protect himself. To keep from being too close, from getting hurt again. But he knew now that risking it all for love was worth the pain.

Robert sat up in bed, turned on the light, fished out his journal and a pen from the bedside table and began to write. He wrote and wrote and wrote, pouring out all his love for her onto the page.

And what if she doesn't love you back? whispered the awful shadow of doubt.

In that moment, Robert knew it didn't matter. Loving deeply was its own reward. He wouldn't ask her for more than she could give.

"WHY DIDN'T YOU TELL ME before that the congresswoman is a knitter and her group meets every Sunday at your restaurant?" Melanie whispered to Coby the next morning. The two of them stood looking out the doors of the kitchen where he worked on Whidbey Island, into the private dining room beyond.

Congresswoman Longren sat at a table surrounded by ladies with basketfuls of colorful yarn at their feet.

"Maybe I would have if I'd known you were hot for her nephew's bod. Can't keep secrets from me and expect to be in the loop."

"So how do I go about this?"

"Never fear, Coby's here. I'll do the honors when they're wrapping up their meeting."

Thirty minutes later, he was introducing her to Pamela Longren and Melanie was shaking her hand. His job done, Coby slipped back into the kitchen.

"It's an honor to meet you," Melanie said. "I work with your nephew, Robert, in New Orleans."

The woman's smile widened. Robert's aunt had the same blue eyes as Robert, the same patrician cheekbones. "Ah yes, he speaks of you often, Melanie."

"He does?" That piece of information took her by surprise.

"Oh my, yes. He calls me once a week like clockwork. I wish my own son kept in touch that often. I'm afraid you frustrate Robert." There was humor in her voice, as if she found the idea an amusing one.

"I do?" Melanie found that hard to believe.

"But in a very good way. Robert's always played it safe. Never taken many chances. You challenge him and he needs that."

"Could I talk to you for a little while? I'd like to learn more about Robert's past."

"Why don't you ask him about it?"

"I did. He won't talk."

"If he doesn't want you to know about his personal life, it's probably not my place to discuss it."

Melanie felt a slight panic. She couldn't let this opportunity slip away. "Congresswoman Longren…"

"Please, you may call me Pamela."

"Pamela, I'm in love with your nephew, but he won't tell me the truth of his cocaine possession charge."

"You know about that?"

"I know he was arrested and you had the charge expunged from his record. He told me he took the rap for someone else, but that's all he would say."

Pamela's mouth flattened into a thin line. "After all these years, after what that man did to him, he's still protecting Jason."

"Who's Jason?"

"I have an appointment in the city this afternoon, but if you're ready to leave the island, we could talk on the ferry."

"Yes, that'd be great. I'll just get my coat and tell Coby I'm going."

Ten minutes later, she and Pamela Longren were sitting at a window on the ferry, sipping hot coffee as it cruised across Puget Sound.

Pamela leaned back in her chair and studied Melanie for a long minute. "I strongly believe you should be hearing this from Robert, but I do know how stubborn and secretive he can be. He has a lot of trouble expressing his emotions. And you made the effort to fly all the way to Seattle and meet me, so I have to believe you must really care about him."

"I love him with every beat of my heart and I think he feels the same way about me. That's why I'm here. To prove how much I love him."

"Did Robert tell you his parents died when he was young?"

"Yes, but he didn't give me any details."

Pamela took a long sip of her coffee. "Robert's mother, my sister Karen, was one of those quiet, solemn women who seem to only see the dark side of life. Even as a kid, she had this gloomy fatalism. Now, as I look back on it, I can't help wondering if somehow she sensed that she would die young."

Melanie sat quietly, waiting for Pamela to continue.

"She met Robert's father, Michael, in college. It wasn't love at first sight or anything like that. It was calm and rational and sensible. They were good together. Both plodding, methodical, intelligent. But motherhood changed Karen. She had an extremely difficult pregnancy with Robert and lapsed into postpartum psychosis. She was put on medication, and for a while she seemed to be all right. Except that she never really bonded with Robert. I never saw a more solemn youngster in all my life. It's like he was born old."

Tears misted Melanie's eyes.

"Michael tried to be supportive of Karen, but he just couldn't understand what she was going through, and he gradually withdrew deeper and deeper into his work."

"Robert told me that his father was a workaholic and his mother was emotionally unavailable," Melanie said. "That he was practically raised by housekeepers."

"It's true." Pamela sighed. "I was wrapped up in my own career and raising my three kids, and I wasn't paying much attention to what was happening in my sister's life. I still feel guilty for that."

"You can't blame yourself."

"I can and I do. In an attempt to shake Karen out of her doldrums, Michael suggested she learn how to sail. Karen loved sailing, so Michael bought her a catamaran. He was happy to see a glimmer of her old self. But it wasn't just sailing that put the sparkle in Karen's cheeks. It was her sailing instructor. All that passion she'd repressed over the years bubbled up in this one grand love affair."

"What happened?" Melanie asked.

"Karen and her lover ran away together, sailing off on an around-the-world adventure, but there was a boating accident and they were both drowned. Robert was just a boy at the time."

Melanie felt her heart breaking for him. "Poor Robert."

"His father withdrew even more. Michael was a diabetic, and in his depression over losing his wife first to mental illness, then to another man and finally to death, he didn't take care of his health. He died of complications from his disease when Robert was twelve. I think if Robert hadn't kept a journal the way he did, he would have ended up in a lot more trouble."

"Robert kept a journal?" What Melanie wouldn't give to read his innermost thoughts during that difficult time in his life.

"As far as I know, he still keeps one."

She tried to imagine how horrible that must have been for Robert, losing both parents at such a young age, but she could not. She'd been lucky. He'd been truly alone in the world, while she'd always had a big, loving family.

"This is the part I regret most of all," Pamela said. "I didn't take Robert in to live with me. I had my own three kids, and at the time my marriage was on shaky ground and my career was taking off. I offered, but he wanted to go live with the Monroes, a family who'd befriended Michael after Karen died. They were eager to have Robert, and it seemed the best solution for everyone. But I don't think I'll ever forgive myself for not insisting he come live with us. If I'd known how things were going to turn out…" Her voice trailed off.

"What happened?"

"Jason Monroe, the father, was chef at a five-star restaurant. He was about thirty when Robert went to live with him and his family. Jason had a wife and two small daughters, and they treated Robert just like he was their own son."

"I'm guessing Jason was the reason Robert became a chef."

"Yes. He was Robert's mentor and taught him everything he knew about the restaurant business. Jason was one of those passionate, creative types—excitable, easily influenced, but with a good heart. Unfortunately, he also had an addictive personality. He worked late hours and hung out with a young, partying crowd, and eventually got hooked on cocaine."

Melanie could guess where the story was headed.

"By this time Robert was eighteen and working in the restaurant with Jason. The owner found cocaine in Jason's coat pocket. It wasn't Jason's first offense, or even his second. If convicted, he was looking at serious jail time. Robert couldn't let the man he'd come to love like a father go to prison, not when he could step up and take the rap for him."

"I can figure it out," Melanie said. She knew Robert so well. Her heart filled with equal parts pride and sadness. She wished she could have been there for him, to help ease his pain and loneliness. "Robert came forward and said he'd been wearing Jason's coat and that the cocaine was his."

Pamela nodded. "When Jason came to me and told me what Robert had done for him, I insisted on getting the arrest expunged from Robert's permanent record."

"When I found out about that, I thought Robert had used his D.A. aunt to cheat the system." Melanie told Pamela, about her own youthful indiscretions with marijuana and how her parents had made her face the music.

"The liar and cheater in this story was Jason Monroe." The Congresswoman shook her head. "In the end, Robert's sacrifices were for naught. Jason got caught with cocaine again."

"How sad."

"It's worse than that. Jason left the family high and dry, and Robert was taking care of them financially. Karen and Michael's death had left him very well off." Pamela toyed with a brown plastic stir straw and did not meet Melanie's eyes. "By this time Robert was twenty-one. He went searching for Jason and found him using cocaine in a crack den. He confronted him, tried to take his drugs away, and Jason attacked him with a razor blade."

"The scar at his temple." Melanie understood why it had been so difficult for Robert to talk about.

"Robert was forced to have Jason committed to the psyche ward for forty-eight hours. It was either that or press charges and have him thrown in jail. But Robert was too loyal to do that. Blind loyalty, that's his weak spot. He's loyal to people he's forged a bond with, even when they don't deserve it."

Melanie couldn't believe how much Robert had suffered. Now she completely understood that dark and brooding undercurrent he struggled to keep from surfacing.

"It tore Robert up inside to think someone he loved so deeply could hurt him like that. Even so, he paid for Jason's rehab, but as I said, it didn't stick. Finally Jason's wife left him, and Robert took care of her and the kids until she remarried a few years later. It took Robert a long time to get past what happened with Jason. He went to grad school and got his Ph.D. in nutrition. But he's been very careful with his affections and his loyalties since. I was so happy when your mother offered Robert the job at the Hotel Marchand. A fresh start is exactly what he needed."

It all made sense. Why Robert had been afraid to express his emotions. Why he equated passion with disaster. All the passionate people he'd known had self-destructed. And yet, in spite of it all, he'd still been willing to give Melanie a chance. He might have been sad and lonely, but he hadn't been afraid to try again. He wasn't a coward. As she had been. Running from love, running from commitment. Afraid to try again after having failed with David.

Robert was a brave man.

Pamela Longren looked Melanie straight in the eye. "I told you all this so you'll understand. Robert has been through so much in his life. He deserves a woman who'll treat him right. I do think he needs a passionate woman who'll balance him out, but he also needs a loyal, trustworthy one who won't screw him over again. He's suffered enough. If you can't give him what he so desperately needs, Melanie, then for God's sake, walk away."

CHAPTER SIXTEEN

MELANIE DECIDED NOT TO apply for the job at La Chère. Coby was right—he was more suited for it, anyway. Besides, she was going home to tell Robert exactly how she felt about him.

Her plane touched down Sunday at midnight, and she hailed a cab to take her home.

Thirty minutes later, exhausted, she slid out of the taxi, stepping into the rain without an umbrella. She never carried one, didn't even own one. She had no doubt sensible, practical Robert owned dozens. If he were here right now he'd pop one up and shelter her from the razor-sharp teeth of the persistent drizzle.

Before she could get into the house, Waffle, who'd been cooped up inside all day by herself, darted out around Melanie's legs.

"Waffle, come back," she called.

If she was really going to keep that cat she would have to get her spayed so she wouldn't try to run away. Darn Robert's hide for making her name the cat, anyway.

The kitten shot down the stairs.

Robert's right, Melanie thought. *I am like Holly Golightly. Chasing a stray cat through the rain.*

"Waffle, come here," she commanded sharply, but being her typical cat self, Waffle ignored her and kept right on going. Melanie went after her.

The roads were slick. A few cars moved slowly down the block.

Waffle reached the cobblestone street underneath a street-lamp at the same moment a black sedan turned the corner. Instantly, Melanie had a horrible flashback to the hit-and-run accident. The car that had slammed into her grandmother's Cadillac had also been a black sedan.

And now it was bearing down on Waffle, who had stopped in the middle of the road to shake rainwater from her paws.

The sedan honked and tried to stop, but the quick application of brakes caused it to fishtail on the wet stones.

"Waffle!" Melanie screamed, and flung herself off the curb.

But it was too late.

"THERE'S BEEN AN ACCIDENT."

"An accident?" Robert repeated groggily into the telephone. He turned on the bedside lamp, swung his legs off the edge of the bed. Bleary-eyed, he glanced at the clock. It was 3:00 a.m. "Who is this? What's happened?"

"Robert, it's Charlotte. I…" Her voice choked and she couldn't speak. Fear grabbed him and shook hard.

"Melanie. Is it Melanie?"

"Yes."

"Where is she?" he demanded. "What hospital is she at?"

"Canal Street Veterinarian Hospital."

"What?"

"Waffle and Melanie got hit by a car, but Melanie refuses to leave Waffle's side. She's bruised and bleeding but she won't go get help herself until she knows Waffle is going to be okay. I can't make her go. I tried but…"

"Where are you?"

"I'm at home. The veterinarian called me and had me talk to her, but she wouldn't listen to reason. Maybe you can reason with her, Robert."

"I'm on my way. I'll call you when I get her to the hospital."

Heart pounding with terror, Robert gathered up his journal and drove, grim-faced, to the veterinarian hospital. He hurried in through the twenty-four-hour emergency entrance and stopped at the reception desk. "Melanie Marchand and her cat, Waffle?"

The veterinarian assistant took him back to one of the examination rooms.

When Robert saw Melanie sitting there in a rocking chair with the unconscious kitten in her lap, tears streaking the dried blood on her bruised cheek, a feeling of anger and helplessness and abject sympathy washed over him.

"Melanie," he whispered, and rushed toward her.

"Robert." She blinked at him and started crying all the harder. "You're here."

"Of course I'm here."

"Waffle got hit by a car."

"I heard." Gently, he reached out a hand to stroke the still, small creature in her lap. "Charlotte said you got hit, too."

"The fender clipped me as I tried to scoop Waffle out of the way of the tire. The vet said if I hadn't been there to block her, the impact would have killed her."

"Don't you think we should get *you* to a doctor?" He met her eyes and tried his best not to cringe at the sight of the gash above the bridge of her nose. "That cut needs a stitch or two."

"I can't go. Not until I know Waffle is going to pull through."

"Charlotte told me you went to Seattle for a job interview."

"I did."

"How'd that go?"

She shook her head. "I never applied."

"Why not?"

"Because I met your aunt Pamela," she said. "She told me everything, Robert. About your parents, about Jason Monroe."

She studied his face and he knew she was trying to gauge his reaction to her news. Instead of closing down, he let his emotions register on his face. He was surprised and relieved and confused and, oddly, happy.

"I lied to you," he said.

"About what?"

"After we made love. When I told you it was just sex. I lied about that."

"I was so hoping you did."

"I've got something I want to share with you," he said.

"You do?"

He extended his journal to her. "I've never shown it to anyone. It says everything I haven't been able to say."

"Oh, Robert, you don't have to do this."

"Yes," he said. "I do."

"Thank you." Her smile was more splendid than any award, any paycheck he'd ever received.

And then Waffle meowed.

ONCE SHE KNEW THAT WAFFLE was going to be okay, Melanie let Robert drive her to the hospital emergency room. While they waited for the doctor, she read his journal.

It started with the day he'd come to work at the Hotel
Marchand and included his growing feelings for her. His
eloquent words painted a richer picture of this man she loved.

Melanie doesn't realize the power she has over other
people. They adore her so much they insulate her from
her mistakes. I used to think she had no management
skills, but the more I watch her, the more I understand
that's not true. Those who work under her are devoted
to her, and she doesn't even have to ask for their loyalty.
I can't imagine what it would be like to fit so well with
those around you that they anticipate your needs.

He believed that about her? He thought she fit well with
others?
And then another entry.

Melanie never plays it safe. She lives life to the fullest.
She might makes mistakes, but by God, she's not afraid
to put herself out there. She makes me realize that *I've*
always played it safe. Never took a risk, reluctant to
gamble. What am I so afraid of?

The day of the infamous turkey skirmish.

This woman makes me crazy. I'm scared as hell I can't
control this anymore. I want her as I've never wanted
another woman. The chemistry is unbelievable. When
I'm around her my pulse revs up, I feel exhilarated in
a way I've never experienced before. Around her smells
are more fragrant, tastes are more flavorful, colors are

brighter. I'm more aware of everything about her, from the slope of her nose, to the set of her determined chin, to the creaminess of her skin. Yet at the same time my mind is completely muddled.

And the day after they'd made love.

It'd be deadly to let her know how I feel. She's like an obsession, an addiction, and that scares of hell out of me. Is this how Jason felt about cocaine? Is this feeling what he was willing to destroy his life over? I can't handle it. Better to hurt her a little now than to destroy us both later.

Melanie looked up at him.

He was watching her with a mixture of anxiety and tenderness.

"Robert," she whispered, but just then the doctor had arrived to stitch up her nose.

While Robert waited outside, she realized how much she wanted out of the hospital so they could go somewhere and discuss what all this meant for their future.

The doctor finished his task just as her family came swooping into the room.

Rats, she thought. Much as she loved them all, she wanted everyone to go away except for Robert.

They were all there—her mother and Charlotte, Sylvie and Renee, enveloping her in their love. She looked around for Robert and saw he'd slipped out the door, giving her time alone with her family.

"You guys didn't have to come out in the middle of night," Melanie said.

"Yes we did," Sylvie told her. "You're our baby sister and we love you to distraction."

"Even if I was put out with you for taking off for Seattle," Charlotte chided.

"What's been going on with you lately?" Renee asked. "What's wrong?"

Anne sat down on the end of the gurney and took Melanie's hand. "Sweetheart, we just want you to know we're here for you always and forever. No matter what problems you're having."

All four of them exchanged worried looks.

"What are you guys talking about?" Melanie demanded.

"It's okay, sweetheart." Anne patted her hand. "You can be honest with us."

"We know the real reason you went to Seattle," Charlotte said. "We know you went to see your drug dealer."

"My what?" Melanie exclaimed, sitting up straighter on the gurney and staring at her family in disbelief.

"There's no shame involved," Renee said. "It happens. We'll help you through it."

"You guys think I'm doing drugs?"

"You're not?" Sylvie asked.

"No, and whatever gave you that idea?"

Her mother and sisters looked at each other, but this time in confusion.

Charlotte was the first to speak. "Remember that day in your apartment when I brought the dress over for the charity auction? I dropped the cup on your answering machine and it played your messages. I heard your "friend" from Seattle say he had some primo stuff for you."

"Coby was talking about primo gossip." They thought she was using drugs?

"Please don't lie," Charlotte said. "I came back in your apartment a few minutes later because I'd forgotten to tell you something, and I overheard you calling him back. You said, and I quote. 'Cocaine, I want everything you've got, all of it.' Are you going to deny that?"

Melanie tried to remember exactly what she'd said in that phone call to Coby. "You took the words out of context."

"Then what was the correct context?" Charlotte asked.

She wasn't going to tell them about Robert's cocaine conviction, Melanie decided. If he wanted them to know, then he could tell them. Now she understood why he hadn't told her the truth about it when she'd confronted him. What was the point if those you loved were ready to assume you were a liar and a drug addict? It felt like a stark betrayal of trust.

"That day you came to see me in the art gallery, you told me you were strung out," Sylvie said. "You looked nervous and distraught."

"I didn't mean strung out on drugs," Melanie declared. Here she was, feeling like the odd man out again. The one who was different. The one who didn't fit.

"What about the rehearsal dinner?" Renee asked. "You substituted crabmeat for the ground turkey and caused a member of the wedding party to have an allergic reaction. Then you caused the fire with your flambé. What other explanation could there be for your actions?"

Melanie hovered on the brink of tears. How could her family refuse to believe her? She loved them so much and yet she felt so misunderstood.

"Tell them the truth, Melanie. Tell them all of it." Robert had come back into the room. A huge sense of relief swept over her.

"Even the part that concerns you?" She was worried that when her mother found out about Robert's cocaine arrest, she would fire him.

"All of it," he repeated.

"Tell it with me," she said, and extended her hand.

He took it, squeezed her fingers tightly.

Anne got up off the gurney and he sat beside Melanie, never taking his eyes from her face. Piecemeal, they told her family everything that had happened.

When they'd finished, her mother and sisters apologized profusely for jumping to conclusions, and asked for her forgiveness. Anne assured Robert his job was not in jeopardy.

"Melanie," Anne said. "I've got something for you." She reached into her spacious leather handbag and pulled out a photo album. "I was working on this and when Charlotte called I brought it along. I thought it might make you feel better."

She handed the album to Melanie.

It was her baby book—chock-full of pictures with decorations and clever comments from Anne. At the back was a family tree of the Marchands and the Robichaux. There were pictures of her father's parents. Melanie had forgotten how much she looked like her grandmother Marie. Black hair and dark-skinned, tall and muscular...

"Oh, Mama, thank you. This is magnificent." Melanie looked at her mother and her sisters, all well put together even though they'd been called out in the middle of the night. All here because they loved her.

She realized now that what she'd mistaken for criticism was actually love of the highest order. Her family had just wanted to help her, and she'd resisted. Determined she was the odd duck, she'd told herself she had to blaze her own path. But it wasn't true.

This was where she belonged.

She was finally, truly home.

"You were a beautiful baby," Robert murmured, peeking over her shoulder at her baby book. "I wish I could have known you then."

She looked into his eyes and he gazed into hers and she was vaguely aware that one by one her sisters and her mother were slipping from the room. "You know me now. It's enough."

"When Charlotte called and said you and Waffle had been in an accident, I was so afraid I could have lost you without ever telling you how much I love you."

She reached up to caress his cheek. "We're okay. Both Waffle and me."

He brought her hand to his mouth and gently kissed her fingers. "We never did get to make up after our fight last night."

"No," she said, "we didn't."

"I'm sorry I yelled at you after the fire. I apologize for the things I said. It was only because I was so worried about you."

"So we had a fight. You know the best thing about having a fight?"

He grinned. "The make-up sex?"

"You got it."

He kissed her then, slowly, deeply, tenderly. "I love you more than you will ever know, Melanie Marchand."

"And I love you, Robert LeSoeur, with every beat of my heart."

EPILOGUE

THE KITCHEN WAS HOT, but Melanie was hotter.

The sweet cherry aroma of salmon LeSoeur filled her apartment kitchen. And the sight of Melanie, wearing nothing but an apron, skimpy red lace panties and ruby stilettos that made her gorgeous legs look ten miles long, filled Robert with a kind of awe. He still couldn't believe she'd agreed to marry him. He could barely believe she'd had the courage to knock down the protective walls he'd built around himself, and open his heart to love. She was something, his impulsive, stubborn, beautiful, accomplished woman.

"Stop staring at my butt and come here, my passionate chef." She turned and slanted him a coy smile over her shoulder. His heart pounded and his body hardened.

Robert needed no more invitation than that.

In an instant, he was by her side. She dished up a bite of her cherry salmon with chestnuts and feta cheese, and held out the spoon to him, one hand cupped underneath to catch any dribbles.

It was another bizarre combination of ingredients from his favorite chef, but the minute the morsel hit his tongue, Robert was in heaven.

"Mmm, that is so good. You are absolutely awesome, Melanie Marchand."

She smiled at him and he felt her wonderful heat warming him from the inside out. She winked saucily.

He grabbed her around the waist and spun her into his arms. "There's just one thing missing," he murmured.

"Something's missing?"

"Yep."

"I don't know how that can be." She started ticking off the ingredients. "Nope, everything's there."

"It needs a little more heat."

"Salmon LeSoeur's not supposed to be spicy."

"But what about Chez Remy's more adventuresome customers? What are they supposed to eat?"

She grinned. "You're turning the tables on me."

Robert smiled back, knowing in this moment his life was utterly and totally complete. "Hey, babe, you know how it is. Some of us like it hot."

From her place on the windowsill, Waffle meowed in agreement.

* * * * *

HOTEL MARCHAND

Four sisters.
A family legacy.
And someone is out to destroy it.

The story continues with

LOVE IS LOVELIER
by Jean Brashear.

If it could happen once…

Anne Marchand is a successful business-
woman who loved her late husband Remy with
all her heart, and no one could ever take his
place. William Armstrong knows that, but
he'll do anything in his power to make Anne
see that it's okay to love again.

Here's a preview!

WILLIAM WAS ON HIS way downtown immediately after Anne left. He'd sent an e-mail last night to Jud Lawson, the attorney who was serving as trustee for his offer on the Hotel Marchand, requesting that the lawyer he'd hired for this one purpose clear time for him as soon as possible today. First thing this morning, there'd been an answer that Jud had pushed all his appointments back and would be available as early as William could arrive.

There were benefits to being a powerful man. William was not averse to trading upon them when needed, and now was such a time. The desperation in Anne's voice last night when she'd spoken of the demand Charlotte had received worried him. Anne didn't want to sell; he knew that. But rather than jeopardize the financial welfare of her daughters, she very well might force herself to accept the loss of Remy's dream. Her dream. At base, he was certain that what she and Remy had wanted, as all good parents did, was to give their children as secure a future as possible. Anne had proven willing to take risks for herself, but he doubted that extended to her girls. If the hotel's future seemed doomed, she would cast aside those dreams in favor of cashing out for whatever she could recoup.

She deserved better. If she had another offer in hand, a decent one with no urgency attached, perhaps she would feel the freedom to hang on for a while, and matters might improve. She and her girls were working hard to steady the hotel's footing, and he would never bet against Anne Marchand.

Especially not when it gave him more time to lend his own influence toward that end. If she wouldn't accept money from him, he could be there to encourage her, and he would. But he also had the ear of suppliers they held in common, and giving them a nudge to offer her more favorable terms or ride with her longer would be easy enough for him to do.

A delicate balance would be required not to trigger a lot of questions that would make the rounds of the hospitality community in New Orleans. He would never want to embarrass Anne in front of her contemporaries, nor did he have any desire for word of his tinkering with fate to get back to her.

Damn it, if she'd just accept a simple, businesslike loan, he wouldn't have to tread such a precarious path.

Of course, none of what was between them had anything to do with business. And it wasn't the least bit simple.

Judith had seen through to the heart of him. If this were any other hotel, he'd be snapping it up with merciless speed. He'd built a thriving chain by having an instinct for timing, efficiency and economy, leveraging himself into putting out the least investment for the greatest return.

He would never have believed the day would come when he'd be guilty of anything as senseless as making this offer, much less enjoying the prospect so much. Despite the potential for disaster, it had been a long time since he had danced this close to the razor's edge.

The woman was making him crazy.

And he was having a ball.

Romantic reads to
Need, Want

International affairs, seduction and passion guaranteed
10 brand-new books available every month

Pure romance, pure emotion...
6 brand-new books available every month

Pulse-raising romance, – heart-racing medical drama
6 brand-new books available every month

From Regency England to Ancient Rome, rich, vivid and passionate romance...
6 brand-new books available every month

Scorching hot sexy reads
4 brand-new books available every month

MILLS & BOON®

M&B/GENERIC RS a

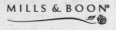

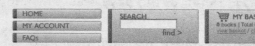

LOOK OUT...

...for this month's special product offer.
It can be found in the envelope containing
your invoice.

**Special offers are exclusively for
Reader Service™ members.**

You will benefit from:

- Free books & discounts
- Free gifts
- Free delivery to your door
- No purchase obligation – 14 day trial
- Free prize draws

THE LIST IS ENDLESS!!

*So what are you waiting for —
take a look* NOW!